The Book of Queens

Joumana Haddad

Interlink Books

An imprint of Interlink Publishing Group, Inc.
Northampton, Massachusetts

First published in 2023 by

Interlink Books
An imprint of Interlink Publishing Group, Inc.
46 Crosby Street, Northampton, MA 01060
www.interlinkbooks.com

Library of Congress Cataloging-in-Publication Data:
Names: Ḥaddād, Jumānah Sallūm, author.
Title: The book of queens / Joumana Haddad.
Description: Northampton, Massachusetts : Interlink Books, an imprint of
Interlink Publishing Group, Inc., 2023.
Identifiers: LCCN 2021062947 | ISBN 9781623717094 (paperback)
Subjects: BISAC: FICTION / LGBTQ+ / General | FICTION / Family Life /
General | LCGFT: Novels.
Classification: LCC PR9570.L43 H33 2022 | DDC 823/.92--dc23/
eng/20220107
LC record available at https://lccn.loc.gov/2021062947
ISBN-13: 978-1-62371-709-4

Printed and bound in the United States of America
10 9 8 7 6 5 4 3 2 1

To my Bachir, whom I called long before he had a name,
whom I'll love long after I've forgotten mine.

I love your sorrow, which is mine as well—
My grief of grieves, all other woes above;
I love your shattered breast, where still your love
Sings on and on—a skylark wild with love.
—DANIEL VAROUJAN
(Armenian poet)

On my rubble the shadow grows green,
And the wolf is dozing on the skin of my goat.
He dreams as I do, as the angel does,
That life is here...Not over there.
—MAHMOUD DARWISH
(Palestinian poet)

Clouds, O clouds
Bless the cursed man walking unto the very end.
Bless me
Teach me the joy of evanescence.
—OUNSI EL HAGE
(Lebanese poet)

All right, century, you have defeated me,
But I will not find in all the Orient
A summit where I can hoist
The flag of my surrender.
—MOHAMMAD AL-MAGHOUT
(Syrian poet)

[1]

QAYAH

(Aintab, 1912 – Beirut, 1978)

Great-grandmother of Qamar
Grandmother of Qadar
Mother of Qana

"She who keeps coming back"

T he **Queen of Diamonds** is resilient, enigmatic, and
self-sacrificing. She goes through many transitions in her
life and keeps taking on new challenges. She can be prone to
anxiety, but she is helped by a natural ability to synthetize
the wisdom gained from her experiences.
Her destiny is ruled by the **Spirit**.

Don't say this world is doomed to darkness,
That eternal life is just a boast,
That the soul is earth and ashes:
I believe in what I must.
—SIBYL ZABEL KHANDJIAN
(Armenian poetess)

Then the Bishop turned to her and said solemnly, as solemnly as his high-pitched voice allowed:

"Repeat after me.

I, Qamar Sarraf, take you, Bassem Barakat, to be my husband, and I promise to love you, to respect you, to be always faithful to you, and never to forsake you. So help me God, one in the Holy Trinity, and all the Saints."

She heard the words as if they were traveling toward her ears from a weird dream, carried by some strange bird's gargantuan wings, ascending slowly like smothered music out of a bottomless pit. They brought back the memory of the well in her grandmother's backyard in Aintab. She loved to listen to the melody of the bucket hitting the water deep down, then coming back up filled, pulled by her grandma's strong arms, spilling a few droplets along the way.

To Qamar, *wet* was a sound, not a sensation. She used to visualize the rusty copper container as a living creature that sang and danced, and even felt tired after too many trips down and up. She was only permitted to sit one meter away from the bricked wall surrounding the well's opening. There she would squat and eavesdrop on the hums and vibrations coming out.

The old widow wouldn't let her stare inside the well.

"Water is the passage of ghosts," she once said to keep her away, even though Qamar knew that ghosts were scary, from the stories that her sister told her every night at bedtime.

"They spy on you, waiting for the slightest glance to drag you down to the dormant circle," her sister warned her. "Whatever you do, never look them straight in the eye."

Just that was enough to frighten the curious girl, and stop her from disobeying. She never drank water from the porcelain pitcher at her grandmother's house so that ghosts wouldn't float in her throat and then slide down into her stomach...

The high-pitched voice continued.

"Repeat after me..."

The bearded Bishop reminded her of one of her father's childhood friends, the "Man who Spoke to Snakes," as she called him. He hypnotized them with his special flute and forced them to sway as he pleased. Whenever he came back to his hometown from one of his long journeys around the world, he'd drop by their house and tell them thrilling stories about his exploits, street performances and the strange, faraway places he had visited. Everyone would be listening to the adventures of his wandering existence mesmerized. Everyone, except for her. She envied him for all the traveling he did, but she did not like him. After every story she would relentlessly ask him the same question.

"But what if the snake did not feel like dancing? What if she was tired and wanted to sleep?"

She.

♦ ♡ ♤ ♧

The snake was a *she*, just like the snake charmer was a *he*. And *she* should dance and dance until *he* decides it is enough, and lets her crawl back into her basket. The venom is there, of course, in her saliva, but she wasn't taught how to use it, she wasn't taught to spit on her oppressor. She was only taught to obey; to feel guilty she was a snake; and more importantly, to imagine that she was the one charming him. The perfect prey is the one unaware it is a prey. The cheating mirrors of the human ego are irresistible.

Was she the dancing snake at the church today, she wondered? A pitiable tool of entertainment for those attending the wedding? There was echo in the cathedral, the kind of echo that makes a person numb. But the discomfort in her feet from the tight shoes she had borrowed from her future sister-in-law was too sharp for any sensation of numbness to prevail. She felt in her neck the burn of all the eyes staring at her, waiting for her to utter the expected words. She finally looked up and spit defiantly.

"I, Qayah Sarrafian, take you, Bassem Barakat, to be my husband…"

An awkward silence followed her vow. Everyone attending the ceremony at the Greek Catholic Cathedral of the Annunciation in Jerusalem noticed she had said a different name. But she wasn't going to allow anyone to intimidate her. Not her. She knew it wasn't the Bishop's fault, though. She was sure that it was Bassem's mother who had asked the poor man of God to drop the "ian" from her family name, and replace her first name, Qayah, with the Arabic one, Qamar.

To say that the zealot Fadwa didn't like that her son's bride was not an Arab, nor a Melkite, would be an understatement. But Qayah was proud of her Armenian heritage, and of all the heaviness that it had engraved in her soul.

She was Qayah Sarrafian, daughter of martyrs Marine and Nazar, adoptive daughter of the late Vartouhi and Grigor. The thick blood of rebelliousness flowed in her veins, along with an addictive liquor called pain.

Marine and Nazar, Vartouhi and Grigor—how she wished they were all here right now, to witness this special day in her life, this "victory." Well, not quite a victory, for the victorious always have choices, and she had none. More a stuck-out tongue in the face of destiny. She was sure that her parents would have also preferred she married someone from their community. But Bassem, whom she had vehemently detested when their engagement was imposed on her, turned out to be a good man, a really good man. Her parents would have approved of him. He was nothing like his wicked mother, who never missed a chance to make her feel "less," unworthy of the Barakat family.

"So you're the seamstress' daughter," she told Qayah scornfully the first time Bassem brought her home to introduce her to his family. "And what does this weird name of yours mean anyway?"

Bassem quickly intervened to defuse his mother's evident hostility.

"It's the name of an ancient moon goddess. And she is my Qamar indeed."

Meaning, "Back off, Mother."

The Barakats were quite ordinary and modest, actually. Not even middle class. But arrogant Fadwa behaved as if they were royalty. That same morning, when she came to visit the bride along with a group of elderly women, forced to do so only by tradition (and *"What would people say about us if we didn't"*), she dropped another lethal dose of her venom.

"Bassem has always loved doing good deeds. Marrying you must be one of them." Qayah ignored her spiteful words, focusing instead on adjusting the lace veil on her head.

♦ ♡ ♤ ♧

Her Palestinian best friend, Negan, kept asking her the thorniest question, ever since Bassem had set the wedding date.

"Are you in love with him?"

"Love is for the living, *habibati*[1] Negan," she persistently replied.

She didn't seek love anyway. Love meant heartbreak. Love meant the forbidden. It meant loss. What she needed was safety, not romance.

"Are you in love with him the way you were in love with Avi?"

"Thankfully, I am not," she answered.

No, she wasn't in love with Bassem. She couldn't be. But after eighteen months of getting to know him during their arranged betrothal, she could tell he genuinely cherished her and would look after her.

That was all that mattered now.

Qayah dreaded only one consequence of this marriage: The physical obligation she'd have toward her husband; what people call "matrimonial duty." She didn't dread it the way a shy and innocent bride dreads what she is yet to discover, and maybe even gradually appreciate. She knew what was expected of her, and she was certain she could never enjoy "it." She understood all too well what a man likes to do with a woman's body. She had learned it the hard way.

In her mind there was one option, one formula only, and it consisted of one who does and one who succumbs. The man takes, the woman surrenders. He feasts, and she waits for him to finish. Every time she envisaged *that* happening between her and Bassem—the groaning, the hammering, the blood, the mess—she wished she could just evaporate.

....

1   Arabic for "my darling."

"A horny man is a famished ghoul," she'd tell Negan repeatedly.

Negan didn't understand where that terror came from, since Qayah abstained from sharing details about her past. She only knew that her friend was an Armenian orphan who had been adopted by Vartouhi and Grigor. Everything else before Jerusalem was a mystery. There are unbreakable silences that one should simply respect, and Negan intuited that Qayah's was one of them. But she also knew how to change her friend's mood with her cheeky sense of humor.

"Well, are you ready to meet the Magic Turtle?" she'd ask her, giggling.

Magic Turtle was how she referred to the penis. Her older married sister had described the apparatus to her one day, and ever since, she portrayed it as a turtle.

"It's apparently a very friendly turtle. If you pat it gently it'll stick out its head and neck and smile at you. Be cautious not to startle it though, or it'll quickly retract and crawl back into its shell."

Qayah would roll her eyes but still chuckle despite herself. Negan was impossibly naughty, but she could make her laugh even at the bluest moments.

The silence in the cathedral was becoming tense. Negan, who was standing next to her, taking her bridesmaid's role very seriously, nudged her with the elbow. Qayah snapped out of her drifting and remembered where she was and why. She looked at Bassem, whose right hand was joined with hers on the Gospel Book, under the Bishop's silk stole. Bassem looked back at her and smiled, as she had anticipated he would. He loved her fiery spirit. The Bishop noticed the groom's smile, took it as a sign of approval, man to man, and only then he went on with the ceremony.

"What God has joined together, let no man put asunder."

♦ ♡ ♤ ♧

She felt a strong urge to turn around and look her mother-in-law in the eye at that moment. Would the vindictive woman make her pay for her insolence? Qayah didn't care. She couldn't wait for it all to be over so she could take off those suffocating shoes.

↩

Jerusalem—Sunday, April 3, 1932

I can't wait to take off these tight shoes…

I look at the men dancing the dabke[2] *around me, at the women in their colorful traditional dresses waving white embroidered handkerchiefs above their heads, and all I can think of is: What am I doing here? How did I get to this point? I don't belong here. I'm an intruder, and always will be. A ghost that has escaped from the realm of the dead and is soon destined to return.*

Am I the only person on the face of this earth who's more frightened to live than to die? More terrified to be happy than to be miserable? I look at the cheerful faces smiling at me, and I feel desperate and alone, like a still drop of water in a running river. How can these people be cheerful? Don't they know this is a scam? That they are only trying to cheat the void? My mind orders me to feel good, but my heart won't obey. Somewhere between the two, the nerves have been cut, communication blocked. This heart of mine is empty, no, it's full—of corpses. They are all crammed in it like worms, eating me up, slowly chewing my organs. Nibble, nibble, nibble, there goes my left lung. Is that why I can barely breathe?

How much does a heart weigh? An empty heart, a non-heart, without the load of love, passion, disappointment, anticipation, affection, ache, excitement, desire, regret, doubt, anger, resentment, warmth, ambition, faith, anxiety, suspicion?

………

2   A folk dance native to the Levant countries.

Without the load of all those we have lost along the way?

An old woman I've never seen before comes and kisses me. I feel a strong urge to wipe the wet sensation of her lips off my cheeks. I feel like slitting my cheeks open with my long painted nails so that they bleed away this lie. Her kiss is a brown stain on my soul, telling me what a dirty fraud I am.

She says, "I hope we'll see your children soon."

I do not want any children. My womb is crammed with corpses, too. No place for a baby there. The worms would eat it bit by bit.

I do not want any children.

Not as long as children can die.

⌐

The day Qayah Sarrafian was born was unlike any other April day Aintab had ever witnessed. The weeks before had been unusually cloudy and rainy, and on that specific evening, spring finally decided to rear its head and a perky moon whispered all the clouds away.

"I will call her Qayah," said Nazar, her father, "because she drew the moon along with her."

Her mother, Marine, protested, and so did her grandmother, the only grandparent that was still alive in the family.

"But Nazar, Qayah isn't a Christian name!"

"But Nazar, it's so uncommon for an Armenian! At least call her Lusin!"

Both women were of the kind hard to oppose. Still, Nazar held his own.

"So what? Look at her. Nothing about her is common!"

In fact, Qayah had quite unusual red hair. Not orangey nor auburn, but a pure, deep, flaming red. Also, she had surprised them by arriving after six consecutive miscarriages. The couple already had two girls, Maria and Hosanna, and a son, Hagop, all of whom were born successively right after their marriage. Then eleven years of health complications hit Marine, and she couldn't keep a baby inside her. When she got pregnant again in 1911, she was certain that this would be her seventh miscarriage.

Qayah proved her wrong.

The baby's siblings, who all had blue-black locks, nicknamed her *Garmeer Klghargeeg*, Little Red Riding Hood. They adored her and catered to her every whim, but she undeniably had a preference for Hosanna, the one who was twelve years older than her. Hosanna cuddled her, fed her and babysat her as if she were her own daughter. Her youngest brother, Nerses, was born one year later, in 1913.

Aintab is Aramaic for "the good spring." Its population consisted of Turks, Arabs, Kurds and Armenians. Nazar was a cobbler and Marine was a seamstress, a very gifted one. Some people called it "magic," the way she could turn a lifeless fabric into a masterpiece of grace; the way she could adapt each dress to hide the flaws of a figure or highlight its assets. Women would come to Aintab asking for her from many neighboring villages.

The couple led a modest life, but so did almost everyone else in their community. Except for Doctor Avediss, who flaunted his enormous belly like a prof of good fortune, no one wore fancy clothes or lived in a big house. The town was known mainly for its cotton and leather works, and many of its Armenian inhabitants had jobs in weaving, shoemaking, cobbling, or similar crafts. It was also a center for commerce due to its strategic location connecting trade routes. Life was simple, as only a humble life can be.

Nazar often brought old shoes home. Townfolk would give them away to him after the shoes had served out their time under people's feet. He had built a special open cabinet for them in the house's spacious, only bedroom, where he and

Marine occupied the timeworn bronze bed, and their kids slept on mattresses spread around them on the floor. The bed was a gift from his mother on his wedding day. It was her own bed and she wanted him to have it. "You were born in it and my wish is for your kids to be born in it too," she categorically stated when he attempted to protest. "Besides, I prefer to sleep on the floor. I feel closer to your father that way."

He never knew his father except through her endless stories about him. Sometimes he felt she invented these tales, then believed them in order to feel less lonely, or to create the life she never had.

Shortly after Nazar was born, his father died from a tooth infection gone bad. The young widow dedicated her whole existence to raising her only son, and when the time came for him to take a wife, she vigilantly took on the task of choosing one for him.

After many inquiries and consultations, she finally settled on an Armenian orphan whose parents had been killed during the Diyar Bakir massacres of 1895. Their twelve-year-old daughter—Marine—had been taken in by the missionaries in the town's all-girls branch of the Aintab College. There she learned how to sew, cook, and trust that she would be *"saved by God's forgiving grace."* Nazar's mother vowed in turn to "save the poor girl from becoming a Protestant." She gave the newlyweds a small piece of land she had inherited from one of her aunts to build a home on. "A new couple shouldn't start their life in the company of an old woman," she said.

Marine hated the shoe cabinet. She had caught a cleaning mania from the three years she had spent with the overly meticulous missionaries and would waste hours scrubbing the ragged shoes in the front yard before allowing them anywhere inside her spotless home. "I don't understand why you like these filthy things," she complained relentlessly. But

Nazar wouldn't listen. He had his reasons, which he couldn't explain to his wife.

There are weaknesses a man can only feel, but never admit. Those "filthy things" had so many stories in them, so many roads taken, and others untaken, so many nice and bad encounters. Every evening he'd bend over the latest pairs he had brought, and spend hours fixing them tirelessly as if he was persuading them back to life. He'd imagine the kind of existence they had withstood, the improbable mountains they had climbed, and the secret confessions they had heard but never got to divulge. If only shoes could speak. If only they could weep or burst out in laughter or scream from pain…

Qayah liked the shoes too. She had a special attachment to them, as she did to all inanimate objects. At such a young age, she couldn't grasp why. She couldn't possibly guess that her early sensitivity brought her to appreciate inanimate objects because they were peaceful, discrete, and low profile. Because they were incapable of suffering. An inanimate object can never be arrogant, or selfish, or tactless, or sore. It is always at the mercy of the living creatures using it. Patient, supportive, forgiving. And when an object breaks down, it doesn't expect living creatures to pity it or sob for its loss. It just quietly disappears.

Ever since she had started walking on her own, Qayah would sometimes sneak in the bedroom when her mother wasn't watching, and try some of the shoes on. There she would spend hours dreaming.

"When I grow up, I want to be a red boot," she declared proudly one evening at the dinner table, while everyone was discussing her brother Hagop's future in cobbling. Nazar almost choked with laughter, but Marine didn't think it was at all funny. "This is all your fault. You and your shoes obsession!"

"Why a boot, Qayah?" her sister Hosanna asked her.

"Because I want to go places."

"But you can go places as a person. Why be a shoe?"

"A person can get tired. When I walk with *Tatiky*, Grandmother, in the fields, she has to stop and rest every half an hour. Shoes don't get tired!"

"True. But then again, why red?"

"Because I have red hair of course!" she answered matter-of-factly.

She would go places all right. Her tiny feet had so many difficult roads ahead to travel, way harder and steeper than any road those old shoes had ever stridden, but she didn't know that yet.

Shoeless she would walk them.

⌒

Aintab—Thursday, April 8, 1915

As of yesterday, I have a new friend. It's a doll, and I named her Yelak, strawberry. My mother made it for me by hand as a gift for my third birthday. It took her seven days of pinning, stitching and snipping. Lastly, she also sewed her a cute pink dress just like the one she had sewed me, and she used red yarn to make her hair look a lot like mine.

She let me watch while she was crafting her. She wouldn't let me use the scissors, but she taught me how to insert the thread in the needle's eye. Every time I'd hand her the threaded needle, she'd tell me, "See this tiny hole, Qayah? It is easier for a camel to go through it, than for a rich man to enter the kingdom of God."

"What's a camel, Mayrik, my Mother?"

"It's a huge animal, sirelis, my beloved."

"Bigger than a horse?"

"Yes, bigger."

"And what's a rich man?"

"Someone whose soul is dead."

"What does dead mean, Mayrik?"
She wouldn't reply.

When Turkish soldiers stormed into their house on that Sunday morning, and arrested her father, Qayah didn't understand what was happening. Her mother was screaming and begging them to spare him, but they wouldn't listen. The militaries tied her father up as if he was a mad dog, forced him to kneel down, and dragged him out on his knees. He was wearing his nice Sunday clothes, as was everyone else in the family. Qayah had her new pink dress on. They were getting ready to go to the nearby Sourp Sarkis Church, for the Sunday morning mass.

"Filthy Christian! No place for you here!"

All Qayah could think of at that moment was her father's knees. They occupied the entirety of her mind and left no space for any other thought.

His knees must be terribly bruised and bleeding from all the dragging. She will bring the magic ointment that her grandmother had used to heal the nasty cut she had once suffered, that time she fell on a spiky rock near the cherry tree.

First, she would wash his knees with hot water and soap, so that the wound doesn't get infected. Then she would spread the ointment and gently blow on her father's knees, because the balm burns a little at first. But only a little. And only at first. Next, she would go fetch the wooden sewing case that her mother kept preciously on the highest shelf in the kitchen. She'd put a chair there and climb it carefully and reach up for the case. She could ask Hosanna to get it for her, but she preferred not to. And Hosanna was too busy crying right now. She would sit next to her father, insert a black thread in the needle, and sew his ripped up black pants. Then everything would be all right again.

Everything.

But her father's strong voice ordered her back to reality.

"If you are going to kill me, at least let me stand up. I don't want to die on my knees." The soldiers ignored Nazar's plea and each one shot him twice in the chest, in front of his wife and kids. He fell right after the first bullet, but they kept on shooting. The same spot again and again. As if it was a competition and they were all aiming at the same target point. The hole in his chest became gigantic, yet his blood took time to pour out. It had been taken by surprise and needed a minute to decide whether it should spill or not. The hole was a red blinding sun staring at Qayah. She covered her eyes with her tiny hands, and only then did she start crying. She knew that no magic ointment could cure such a hole.

Qayah cried and cried. She would never really stop crying, from that moment up until her last breath.

And she never wore pink from that day on. Pink became the color of tears. The color of a father left behind. Of a home left behind. Of a tomorrow she could never catch up with.

~

Aintab—Sunday, April 25, 1915

I am stumbling on people. They are everywhere; the road is paved with bodies. Is this a game they are playing? But if it's a game, why is everybody else screaming and weeping? Walking on people is not a fun game. They look terrifying under my feet. Especially their faces. With each step, I expect them to shriek, but they don't. They just lie there, as still as rocks. They must be very strong, to be able to bear the weight of all those who are marching on them without moving.

A strange man once came to our village. He had funny clothes and a round shaved head. He told us he could walk on fire. He said he didn't feel anything. Then he showed us his blistered feet.

The skin of their soles was black and thick, like charcoal. I kept having nightmares about those feet for many weeks afterward. Will my shoeless feet become like his?

Come on, stand up, all of you. Enough of this horrible game already!

I miss my Papa, my Hayrikes. I miss my Grandma, my Tatikes, too. Why did we leave them behind? Mama told me that they were never coming back. "Never ever," she said.

Is it my fault? Did I do something wrong?

I'm hungry, but there's no food. I'm eating grass. It tastes bad. It is covered with dust and I think there was an insect on it too.

It is so hot. I am dry and tired. I think I will sleep a little.

Goodbye, Tatiky. Goodbye, Hayrik.

⟶

Immediately after Nazar's killing, Marine was ordered to evacuate the house. She covered her husband's body with a white blanket, packed up all the food she could find, and took her five kids on a journey to flee the danger zone. They marched along with other women, children and a few old men from Aintab and neighboring Armenian villages. Decomposing cadavers crammed the streets, like leaves that have fallen from trees.

Those who die on us never leave, even when they are left behind. Before her departure, Marine laid down the image of her husband's corpse in her memory, next to her parents'. Memories are like morgues: Endless rows of drawers that we sometimes reopen to check up on our dead. *You've grown so much, my beloved. This new haircut really suits you. Of course I haven't forgotten about you! I was just too busy getting prepared to die myself.* We wink at them, then we close back the drawers and leave. But only for a short while. We know we will join them soon in someone else's memory.

The group traveled through the Syrian desert on foot, trying to make it safely to Aleppo, where Marine had a distant relative. Qayah's mother dressed her two brothers as girls, in order to safely cross the dangerous areas, as the Turkish were systematically killing all the males. But they hadn't yet traversed the precincts of Aintab when a soldier noticed fourteen-year-old Hagop's nascent mustache, and shot him instantly. He wouldn't allow Marine the time to properly say goodbye to her firstborn son. He pitilessly dragged her away from the corpse of Hagop, who lay peacefully in his blue dress, a wounded bird wrapped up in a cloudless sky. She was embracing him like a Madonna Addolorata, but the soldier forced her to get up and keep walking.

⸺

That same evening, when the dense darkness of the desert nights fell on the convoy, she suddenly felt an unfamiliar presence near her. A man's voice whispered something unintelligible in her ear. Marine couldn't see who it was, and got scared at first. But the voice was warm and kind. The stranger thrust something in her hands, gently patted her shoulder, then moved on. As a ray of moonlight fell on his shadow while he was hurriedly walking away, she recognized, from his clothes, that he was a Turkish soldier. Stunned, she checked what he had given her—it was the blue dress that Hagop was wearing, stained with his blood and sweat, and a half-full goatskin water pouch. Marine inhaled the smell of her son and started crying. She didn't know what was making her cry more: the unbearable loss of her child, or the discovery of a humane heart amid such madness.

On that journey in hell, Marine was raped more than once by various soldiers, and nearly died. Hosanna was raped too, on the second day, but the girl's frail physique couldn't handle

♦ ♡ ♤ ♧

it. Her heart stopped right in front of Qayah's eyes. She had the lower part of her dress lifted up and covering her head, so Qayah could not see her face at the moment she perished. She only saw the parted legs, and the blood that was dripping in between them, from that "shameful part of the body" that her mother always commanded her and her sisters to hide.

That shameful part of the body where the carnage begins.

That shameful part of the body where suffering and ecstasy merge.

That shameful part of the body where all secrets are kept.

That shameful part of the body where all roads converge.
That
shameful
part
of
the
body
where
the
dead
resurrect.

It was a training in loss for Qayah. One that would seal her fate irreversibly. Gaghant baba[3] and fairy tales with happy endings were forever gone. After many days of wandering under a pitiless sun, they still hadn't reached Aleppo, because the Turks were driving them through arduous paths to make their journey harder. Indirect routes through mountains and wilderness areas were deliberately chosen in order to prolong their ordeal.

Gradually the convoy became a third of what it initially was, losing people like cropping flies along the way. Death had gotten so common that it didn't generate any reaction

....

3   Santa Claus

anymore. Not even mothers' tears. No sight is crueler than that of people who have become accustomed to horror. Stripped of their humaneness, a cost they could no longer afford, they went on like zombies, dragging the heavy shadows of their martyrs behind them.

Thirst was meaner than hunger. It was a miracle that Marine's remaining three kids had survived. The water pouch the soldier had given her had quickly dried up. *"Tzaravem, I'm thirsty!"* the children kept imploring, and Marine wished she could cut her wrists open and give them her blood to drink. But blood, she knew, didn't quench thirsts.

It only quenched hatred.

Hers were the only kids still alive in the group, and the adults took turns carrying the youngest two when they became too exhausted. The latter were the ones that Marine was mostly worried about. Nerses was struggling, but little Qayah was tough. She seldom complained. Ever since Hosanna's passing, it was as if she had moved irreversibly into another dimension, another reality, where she was a witness of horrors, against her own will. The deep dark circles under the girl's eyes were a voracious black abyss swallowing the Armenian people.

Midway to Aleppo, Marine suddenly stopped by the side of the road, took her breasts, out and started squeezing them frenetically, imagining she could get milk out of them for her children. She had stopped breastfeeding Nerses less than six months ago. Maybe she wasn't completely dried up yet?

"The poor woman has gone crazy," said another deportee.

A Turkish colonel noticed the scene, as he was checking the caravans, parading like a peacock atop his horse. He was hunting for sex slaves.

"Bunu, this one," he called out to one of the gendarmes, pointing his finger in her direction, and the soldier immediately went and started pushing her with the back of his rifle.

♦ ♡ ♤ ♧

She didn't resist. As if she was in a nightmare, incapable of getting out, or deciding the turn of the events.

"You come with me," the Colonel instructed her, with authority.

She just nodded.

⌐

The Syrian Desert—Monday, May 3,1915

I am afraid.

I am afraid. I am hungry. I am thirsty. Where is Hagop now? Why isn't he teasing me or picking flowers for me like he used to?

I see soldiers with rifles everywhere. To the left. To the right. In the front. In the back. They are shouting at us. They hate us. Why do they hate us? What did we do to them? Why do they keep ripping women's clothes and ordering them to lie down? The women yell and cry, but the soldiers don't seem to mind. They did that to Mother and to Hosanna too.

Why did Hosanna stop moving? Is she asleep? No, she can't be. Hosanna never goes to sleep before I do.

Mama said that Hosanna was dead. Hagop too.

What does dead *mean, Mayrik?*

The soldiers are pushing those who are lagging behind with the rear of their weapons. Walk. Walk. Walk. Are we in a race? If we are, where is the finish line?

I don't think there is a finish line.

Goodbye, Hagop. Goodbye, Hosanna.

⌐

The Colonel let Marine keep Qayah with her. Qayah only. Her two other remaining children were to continue their way to Aleppo with the group. She told Maria the name of her relative there, implored her to watch over her baby brother, and promised to join them, along with Qayah, as soon as she could. She hugged them long and hard. Did she know then she was never to see them again?

A mother always knows.

Does power corrupt human beings, or do the latter have latent beasts inside of them, waiting for the slightest opportunity to wake up and start slaughtering their fellow humans? Are all people butchers in disguise?

As she was crying and saying goodbye to her siblings, Qayah wished she could transform into a shoe. A shoe that would run after them. A shoe that would carry her mother away, far away from the evil man. A shoe that would just sit by the side of the road and wait for all the sleeping people to wake up.

A shoe, lifeless, that would feel nothing.

The horrors that Marine witnessed subsequently in the Colonel's villa in Adana, from daily beatings to routine rapes, made her feel at times that she was paying, alone, the price of being an Armenian woman. But she knew she wasn't the only one to pay that heavy price.

The only things that kept her from killing herself during those days were the terror of leaving Qayah behind and the prospect of reuniting with her two other kids. Often, at night, when her injured vagina was too sore for her to fall asleep, she'd picture herself cuddling them in order to bring herself to slumber. She knew she had to take Qayah out of that awful place where little girls as young as eight were being abused and raped. She just didn't know how.

Like many other sex slaves during that time, Marine got pregnant from the Colonel and gave birth to a baby on February 20, 1916. It was practically snatched out of her womb and immediately taken away. Elmas, one of the palace's cooks, was a kindhearted young Turkish woman who had become her only friend. She always brought her and little Qayah sweets and fruits in secret. She told Marine that the baby was a boy and that he would be named Aslan. She clandestinely came back with the infant later that night, gently opened Marine's blouse, and placed the newborn on his mother's bare chest.

"*O kokunu gerektiği,*" she whispered to her. *He needs to smell you.*

Turkish was a language that Marine, like the majority of Armenians under Ottoman rule, understood and spoke very well.

"This way he'll never forget you. Our mothers' skin is our only real homeland."

The baby was a redhead, just like her Qayah. Marine knew how big the risk was that Elmas had taken, and felt grateful. The poor woman could be killed for far less. As Marine felt the boy's heartbeats synchronizing with hers, she didn't know whether she loved him or hated him, whether she wanted him to remember her smell or she needed to forget his. It didn't matter anyway. Elmas had to take him away shortly afterward. Marine asked her to put a lock of his hair in the steel locket that hanged around her neck.

The locket was a gift from Nazar a few months after Marine had given birth to Qayah, and she had religiously kept ringlets from all her children's hair in it. She still remembers every detail of their conversation the day he gave it to her. She had pouted at first, as she was expecting gold jewelry. She had, after all, given birth to a new baby after eleven years of hardship! It was a big deal, if not a miracle. She knew he couldn't buy her a substantial item, like a necklace or a bangle, but she would have been content with a simple pair of golden earrings. However, Nazar assured her that this particular kind of steel was much more valuable, and that it soon would be more expensive than gold.

The day Qayah was born, he asked his friend, the snake charmer, to bring him something special for his wife from England, where the man was heading aboard a commercial steamship exporting cotton to Europe. The ship was to leave from Mersin, traverse the Mediterranean Sea making stops in different European cities, then cross the strait of Gibraltar and navigate the Atlantic Ocean all the way up to England. Eight months later, around Christmas of 1912, the man came back to Aintab, and proudly handed Nazar a steel chain and locket. "Harry, a metallurgist I have befriended in Sheffield, has made them especially for me, from a new material he had recently invented. It is not just any steel. It is steel that never rusts!"

Nazar faithfully repeated all of his friend's words.

"This is the Superman of all metals, Marine! Not only it doesn't corrode, just like gold, but it will last forever, like my love for you!"

Right after Elmas cut a lock of Aslan's hair and placed it in the locket, she carried him off and Marine was never to see him again. She wasn't aware that Qayah, who was sleeping on the ground next to her, was awake, intently observing and listening, etching every single detail of that scene in her mind.

In her *genes*.

Only two days after the delivery, despite her exhaustion and the heavy bleeding, Marine tried to escape with Qayah. The Colonel sent his soldiers after them, and they killed her in the outskirts of Adana, after taking turns raping her.

"Run, Qayah, run!" her mother kept yelling while the brutes were thrusting their bodies on hers.

But Qayah couldn't bring her feet to run. She just hid behind a thick bush, and heard it all. The sound of fabric being slit, the rude slaps on the naked flesh, the pitiless hammering, the men's vulgar laughs...

Then it was over.

♦ ♡ ♤ ♧

They left, suddenly, and only a ruthless silence remained. Qayah finally took a glance. She would never forget the face of her mother lying on the ground with eyes wide open. She would never forget her bare wounded feet.

She would never forget the rest either.

A Kurdish merchant found the little girl that same evening, lying next to her mother's corpse. He had a daughter her age, and he felt pity for her. He gave Qayah something to eat, then hid her inside a carpet in his carriage and took her with him to Aleppo.

At first Qayah refused to leave her mother's side.

"What if she woke back up?" she kept repeating, like a mantra.

"She won't wake up, my child."

"Why?"

"Because she's dead."

"What does *dead* mean?"

Just like her mother, the merchant wouldn't reply. But he eventually convinced her to leave with him. She covered her mother's face with Hagop's dress, the only thing that Marine took with her when they had escaped. She unfastened the steel chain and locket from around her mother's neck, and put it around hers. Once in Aleppo, the man left her in an orphanage.

Qayah would never forget the name of the Turkish Colonel.

Beshir Kizlar Agha.

Adana—Tuesday, February 22, 1916

Run, Qayah, run!

I keep telling myself that. Just keep on running, Qayah. This road will eventually come to an end.

Nothing. What happiness it must be to be nothing. No barking dogs, no howling winds, no savage nights. I have come to understand exactly what I am feeling. I'm not longing to disappear. It's just that my soul yearns for the time before me, the time when I wasn't even here yet.

The peaceful state of "nonbeing" instead of the messy "ceasing to be."

Existence is an excruciating construct. I envy what does not know it exists. Those are the only real innocents. All the unaware, inanimate objects that surround us, most of which we have made ourselves, with our hands and our machines. Oh the serene life of the lifeless!

Why couldn't I have been born a pebble, or a box, or a metal chain?

Better yet than objects, are ideas and concepts. Big words are invented, endless analysis are made, and even disastrous wars are fought for something as intangible as "justice," "freedom" or "responsibility." The human race is a joke. A tasteless one.

I would have loved to have been born as the absurd idea of "victory."

Run, Qayah, run! This road is bound to shed you soon. And you'd better stop crying: From now on you shall be called an orphan and orphans must swallow their tears. Or else, they'd drown the whole planet.

Goodbye, Mayrik.

⁓

Vartouhi and Grigor were a kind, middle-aged Armenian couple with no children, originally from a village in the Moussa Dagh region of southern Turkey. They had managed to escape to Aleppo in 1916 after a year of privations and torture in Deir El Zor, a city southeast of there, where many Armenians had been forced to head following the start of the genocide. Vartouhi was a seamstress, and Grigor had set up

♦ ♡ ♤ ♧

a small thrift shop in Aleppo from the money that Vartouhi had managed to hide in her hair and mouth the day they were kicked out of their home by Turkish soldiers.

The First World War had ended only a few months ago, and people were feeling optimistic. The couple had been talking about adopting a child survivor for quite some time when one day, they finally decided to make the move and went to visit the German orphanage for Armenian children in Aleppo. They immediately noticed Qayah. Not only did she have uncommon red hair, but she also was the only kid who was not playing. She just sat there, detached, observing the other children.

Orphanages are temples for choked up tears. That was Vartouhi's thought when she walked into that forsaken place. All the kids seemed to have the same engorged eyes, and that was the first, almost only thing one might notice in their otherwise effaced faces. Eyes filled with "whys." Twirling whys, welding like wire fences between the universe and them.

At first the couple thought Qayah was merely three or four years old because of her fragile constitution and delicate features. She was small for her age and they were astounded to find out she was almost seven.

"*Geghetsik aghtchik, inche'h anounet,* what's your name, beautiful girl?" Vartouhi asked her. The woman didn't expect an answer. Many Armenian orphans couldn't remember their names, birthdates, or the places they came from. Their whole past had become hazy in their minds.

Trauma, people call it. But truth is that forgetfulness, if successfully achieved, can be the fastest cure for misery. Wipe the slate all clean, then start anew. But how can the living dead forget? More importantly, how can the living dead start anew? The tunnel was unavoidable, and it was watching all those kids like a hungry predator waiting for the first opportunity to ambush and devour them.

"My name is Qayah Sarrafian, and I was born in Aintab on April 11, 1912, daughter of Nazar and Marine. My father is a cobbler and my mother is a seamstress," the little girl would proudly reply, just the way her late sister Hosanna had taught her to, ever since she had first learned to speak.

Hosanna used to tease Qayah about the first word she had ever said. It wasn't *Mayrik* or *Hayrik*, Mama or Baba, like most babies; not even Hosanna, or *Kuyrik* Sister. Qayah's first word was *lolik*, Armenian for tomato. She loved tomatoes so much as a toddler that, whenever Hosanna had to leave her and she'd start crying, she'd give her a tomato to nibble on. That would calm her down instantly. She had started speaking earlier than all of her siblings, at barely fourteen months. And by the time she was two, Hosanna had already taught her to say several full sentences. She could even form some on her own.

Qayah held Vartouhi's disconcerted gaze without blinking. There was something inexplicable about her. She wore the sage expression of an old soul who had no more demands of the world; as if she had lived and died many times already, had little air left in her besieged chest and little feathers left in her burnt-out wings.

The woman got goosebumps when she heard the orphan's last words. "My mother is a seamstress," echoed in the seamstress' ears like a message from above. "Let's take her home," she whispered in Grigor's ear.

And that was all it took—motherly love at first sight. Vartouhi felt her womb alive for the first time in her life, as if she had given birth to the girl herself. Some become mothers by the burgeoning of the flesh; others by the pounding of the heart.

They picked Qayah up and took her home, just like people in times of peace would pick up a kitten or a puppy from a shelter.

♦ ♡ ♤ ♧

After only a few weeks of reserve, Qayah surrendered to the couple's sincere affection and opened up to them. Less than six months after their first encounter in the orphanage, she started calling them Mama Vartouhi and Baba Grigor, without them even asking her to do so. But they waited in vain for her to talk about the past. It was buried deep in a tightly sealed box and the tightly sealed box was buried deep in her memory and her memory was buried deep in the mysterious steel locket she wore around her neck, the one thing she never took off.

She did not need a memory anyway. She only needed a new story.

And a new pair of shoes.

When finally they managed to issue her an identity card, they chose to let her keep her original family name as well as her original parents' names. They felt it was the least they could do out of respect for her deceased mother and father.

Qayah Sarrafian, daughter of Marine and Nazar, born in Aintab, on April 11, 1912.

A fallen angel between two interminable nights.

⟶

Aleppo—Sunday, March 9, 1919

Between life and me there are walls that never became a home,
Larvae that never turned into butterflies,
And a broken time-machine that will always keep us apart.

Between life and me there are rivers that never shall meet,
Days where people have disappeared,
And a circular wind that scatters our words.

Between life and me there's this valley of death
And the knife of despair

Slowly carving the wooden crib
Where I shall finally lay down my tired heart.

Qayah loved the bed that Baba Grigor had made for her. But she hated the barriers he had added on all four sides to keep her from falling out. Her sleep was so turbulent that he would unmistakably find her lying on the floor every single morning. So he ended up installing the rails.

She had a recurrent nightmare in which she'd see herself sinking into her grandmother's well. The ghosts would catch her and take her into a side cave where her mother would be sitting on the ground, next to a boy she hadn't seen before, who had red hair just like her. Soon she'd realize that the woman wasn't her real mother. She looked like Marine, but she had black hands, as if they were made of tar. She would put those hands around Qayah's neck and start squeezing. The boy would laugh hysterically while jumping and clapping his hands. Then Marine would say to him, "Come, Aslan! Help me kill her!" and Qayah would wake up gasping for breath.

She'd also often dream about her father, grandmother, sisters and brothers. Not slain, not forever lost, but laughing and playing with her. On those mornings, she wished that she hadn't woken up at all.

And so, for a little over a year she lived with her adoptive family. But things in Aleppo weren't going well for them. The high hopes that immediately followed the end of World War I turned out to be mere illusions, and people everywhere were struggling. The thrift shop business wasn't thriving as Grigor had expected it would, and the family was living off Vartouhi's small and irregular sewing jobs.

Also, Grigor's health was gradually deteriorating. He had heard that an influenza epidemic had broken out worldwide.

He thought he might have caught it, too. But he made sure not to share his suspicion with his wife and daughter. He could feel his vigor slowly but surely wither away, and he abstained from hugging Vartouhi and Qayah, or breathing too close to their faces. "This damn cold," he'd say to reassure them every time they heard him cough. To make things worse, the city wasn't safe enough for them. The policemen and the guards were still pursuing the Armenians and arresting all the refugees who did not have permits, imprisoning them and resending them to Deir El Zor.

Grigor received word that two of his cousins had made it safely to Jerusalem, and he took the decision to sell back the shop and head there with his wife and adoptive daughter.

"At least we'd have family nearby," he told the reluctant Vartouhi. "Everyone says Jerusalem is such a spectacular city, and you'd be living in the Holy Land!"

He knew she couldn't resist the last argument, being such a devout Christian. Whenever he wanted to convince her of something she resisted doing, or win over an argument with her, he'd pretend an angel visited him in his sleep and told him this or that. After numerous years of marriage, there was a cohort of angels in their ménage, and Grigor was so ingenious that he would not forget the weird names he had invented for each one of them. Vartouhi never suspected he was lying. Not because she was naïve or stupid, but because she was so sincerely pious that she couldn't even conceive someone lying about such matters. The day she finally admitted to herself that she was having problems getting pregnant, she started asking him the same question, every morning.

"Well, did *Clamarama* tell you something about us having a child?"

Clamarama, the alleged angel of fertility.

"Not yet, *sirelis*, my beloved." Grigor would answer.

"Can you at least ask him about that the next time you see him?"

"I surely will," he assured her. "But just so you know, yesterday *Parkasina*, visited again.

Parkasina, the alleged angel of nourishment.

And she told me you should prepare *Vospov Kufta*[4] more often."

Obviously, these patties made of red lentils, bulgur, and onions were Grigor's favorite dish, and his wife's least favorite. But Vartouhi never contested, never questioned, never even wondered why the angels wouldn't visit her for a change.

The playful but kindhearted Grigor felt guilty at first. But the allure of the "easy winning-zero nagging" method quickly wiped out any remorse from his conscience. Grigor also made sure she didn't tell any priest.

"They said they would stop visiting if you did."

⌒

Timazan, the angel of travelers, ended up making a revelation to Grigor about their need to go to Jerusalem, of course, so the family took the train one morning and never looked back. Once there, they settled in one of the quarters of the Armenian Convent, near the Sourp Hagop Church, the Church of Saint James. And there, for the first time in a very long while, they finally felt safe. Gone were the dreadful bayonets of the gendarmes. Gone were the shouts to walk—*Yürümek!*—which struck them like lightning and filled them with terror. Gone, most of all, were days of wandering in the desert.

But the decaying corpses remained and would never be gone. They were to become an eternal reminder to all

....

4   A traditional Armenian dish made with red lentils.

♦ ♡ ♤ ♧

Armenians, living or yet to be born, that this world was just one big death row.

The trick is to forget it.

Or to decide for yourself the time of the execution.

↩

Aleppo—Friday, April 16, 1920

Is misery a blessing or a curse? I often ask myself this question.

But what's the point in knowing the answer? What would it change in this horror ride? If misery were indeed a blessing, would the doomed suddenly start to feel privileged? Would a father brag about how lucky he is to have lost a child to famine?

And if privilege were a curse, would the blessed ones feel miserable for having been born so advantaged?

Luck is always against us. Even when it stands by our side. Because if we were shrewd, we'd know very well that it won't last. And right there in the middle of our glory, we will start panicking, and feeling depressed, about the inevitability of losing it.

The fear of sadness after joy. The fear of disenchantment after faith. The fear of failure after victory.

I have found the perfect remedy for that fear.

Ah, the incommensurable magnificence of total desperateness.

↩

She had never seen a refrigerator before, nor even heard of it. The first time she discovered its existence, was at Negan's house. Negan had been her best friend ever since she had arrived in Jerusalem, and they often spent their afternoons together. Negan's mother was an Armenian of Persian origins, and Negan would often brag that her name, meaning "good destiny" in Persian, was that of a brave female warrior who fought against the Arab Invasion of Persia. She never knew her mother though, who had died giving birth to her. This, along with the Armenian connection, cultivated an instant complicity between the two girls.

Negan's father, Shafik, who was Palestinian, was heartbroken and inconsolable for a long time. He had met his wife when they were both seventeen, during one of the trips he took with his own father to Isfahan, Persia, and he got severely love-struck. Shafik was a trader, like his father before him, and he would be gone for weeks, even months sometimes.

"I don't think I could go on living without her, Father," Shafik said. "Could we bring her back to Jerusalem with us?"

"Why not?" Shafik's father answered.

So he immediately visited the girl's parents and asked for her hand. His request was rather easily granted, since Shafik's father and the girl's father had already met during previous trips, and they did business together.

Shafik's mother was stupefied by all this. She had said goodbye to a husband and a son, and only two months later she was welcoming home a husband, a son, and a daughter-in-law.

After his beloved's passing, Shafik eventually found himself forced to remarry, as he needed someone to take care of his three daughters. But his second wife was the typical, evil, two-faced stepmother. It didn't help that she never managed to have any kids of her own with him. Her bitterness nourished her wickedness, and vice versa.

Ammo, or Uncle, Shafik, as Qayah called him, had become wealthy as a trader. Whenever he came back from his trips, he'd bring gifts to his wife and children, and he never forgot to also bring something for Qayah. *"Not all rich men have dead souls*, Mayrik," Qayah comforted her departed mother. Shafik was also well read, and he would tell them incredible stories and facts about the world.

♦ ♡ ♤ ♧

One hot summer afternoon, Ammo Shafik brought with him a white rectangular container, installed it in the living room, sat everyone on the floor around it and showed them what it did.

"It's a Frigidaire!" he announced proudly at the end of the demo.

Qayah had no idea what he meant by that. Which name was it—*Refrigerator* or *Frigidaire*? But she was ashamed to ask Negan. She felt embarrassed that her friend could read and she couldn't. Mama Vartouhi was too attached to her to send her to school. Qayah even had to beg whenever she wanted to go to Negan's house. Most of the time it was Negan who would come by.

Before moving the refrigerator to the kitchen, Shafik let Negan and Qayah thrust their heads inside it, and the two girls were amazed by the coolness that pervaded them.

When Qayah got back home on that day, she was impatient to tell Baba Grigor about the marvelous invention. He loved to hear about Ammo Shafik's latest acquisitions. But it was too late. Grigor had passed away, succumbing finally to the bacteria that had consumed him slowly during the past four years. He hadn't caught the infamous Spanish Flu, like he had initially thought, but tuberculosis. Both were deadly in those days, but TB was more gracious: It gave people more time.

Vartouhi insisted on burying her husband in a white coffin, despite the tradition stipulating that white was reserved strictly for deceased children, because they were angels. "He was an angel too," she declared. "That is why so many angels kept visiting him—Clamarama, Parkasina, Timazan...all of them."

The wailing women who were gathered around Vartouhi thought that heartache was making her hallucinate. As the convoy proceeded toward Sourp Hagop Church under an unforgiving August sun, the white casket resting on men's sweating shoulders, Qayah wished her adoptive father had been laid in a refrigerator instead, so that he wouldn't feel the heat.

"Poor Baba Grigor. It must be suffocating to be under the ground."

No, Qayah. Poor you. Poor us. For it is far more suffocating to be above it.

⌐

Jerusalem—Sunday, August 3, 1924

Sometimes I feel fortunate I cannot read.

Words are cutting enough when they are said. Written, they could be deadly. I am sure of that.

Those who can read aren't allowed the bliss of amnesia. They keep running into their pain in the written memories of those who survived to tell the story.

The day my father died, I became blind.

The day my brother died, I became deaf.

The day my sister died, I became mute.

The day my mother died, I became paralyzed.

I am still waiting for the roaring in my brain to stop. Only then will I be able to forget. Only then will I have the right to be discarded.

Only then will I stop feeling so afraid and lonely.

Maybe.

Goodbye, Baba Grigor.

⌐

It wouldn't have happened, and they most probably would've never met, if it weren't for Fire.

That afternoon, Qayah had gone to deliver a new dress to Oum Rami,[5] who had commissioned it to wear for her son's

---

5   Arabic for "Mother of Rami." It is a custom in the Arab world to designate the mothers in relation to their first-born sons.

upcoming wedding. It was a lovely dress, one that Qayah had helped Vartouhi sew and embroider. The seventeen-year-old had become a quite skilled seamstress herself. In fact, many of the Christian Quarter's wealthy women were beginning to ask specifically for Qayah whenever they wanted something out of the ordinary.

Vartouhi felt increasingly rewarded. She had managed to raise a kind and hardworking young woman. Grigor would have been so proud. After he died, the mother and daughter were left to get by on their own, which they did rather well thanks to Vartouhi's tailoring skills. Qayah didn't just pick up those skills, she took them even further. She had an unusual flair for fashion, as if she was born to breathe life into any piece of fabric.

Actually, she was.

Oum Rami's dress had been quite a challenge, though. The short and plump woman had the constitution of a square box. No waist to be seen, no neck either: just one block of flesh, equal in height and width, topped by a peculiarly small head. It was as if her head was a tiny light bulb, screwed right into the middle of her wide shoulders. Whenever Oum Rami turned her head to the left to look at something, Qayah imagined that the light bulb was being unscrewed and Oum Rami's head would fall off.

Vartouhi was desperate, so Qayah took on the challenge. She decided to sew the woman an Abaya to hide the lack of curves in her body, with a V-neck collar to create the illusion of a neck. She compensated for the absence of a pattern in the cut with an elaborate and colorful embroidering that went from the middle of the collar all the way down to the hem. It divided Oum Rami in two, and that was exactly what Oum Rami needed, Qayah kept thinking amusingly while working on the outfit. Her efforts were rewarded. When the woman tried the Abaya on, she was ecstatic.

"*Yeslamu idayki ya binti*, thank you!"[6] Oum Rami thanked her effusively.

Qayah was already walking back home from the satisfied client's house when she heard people shouting in the distance. She always had a fast, almost military-style, walk. She could never tread slowly and lasciviously like other young women did. To her, walking was a way to get as quickly as possible from point A to point B. Period.

Life was the same. Except that "as quickly as possible" was taking longer than she secretly wished for.

The closer she got to home, the louder people's screams were becoming. First she noticed the black, thick smoke. Then she spotted the tip of the flames. Then she saw the blaze bursting out of the modest apartment she shared with Mama Vartouhi.

She immediately understood.

She asked no questions. She didn't cry. She just sat there on the dusty ground and calmly observed the fire eating away the only family she had left.

Can all of this happen to one person?

Yes, it can.

Qayah didn't realize she was trembling. Two gentle hands wrapped a blanket around her shoulders and patted her back. She looked up.

That's when she saw him for the first time.

☞

Jerusalem—Friday, December 6, 1929

If everything that happens is meant to be, then why do we even trouble ourselves waking up each morning? If it's all meant to be,
....

6   Arabic for "may your hands be safe my daughter," a form of saying "thank you."

why try so hard?

There are no unpredicted adventures to live, no challenges to win, no trials or errors to learn from. Can't we tear up even one page from that book where everything is written in advance? Can't we change one single word?

Only if —I would replace "death" with "deliverance."

Goodbye, Mama Vartouhi.

↩

It wouldn't, couldn't, shouldn't have happened. And yet, it did.

Isn't love the master of all road accidents?

He was a Jew, and Jews were a no-no.

"They are evil and they crucified Jesus," Vartouhi, the devout Christian, always said.

"They are evil and they want to take our land," Ammo Shafik, the fervent Palestinian, always said.

But Avi was not evil. How could anyone with such amber-green eyes be evil?

Avi did not crucify Jesus. How could anyone who wouldn't even shoot a bird crucify Jesus?

Avi wanted nobody's land.

Avi just wanted her.

Vrd dvm, Hebrew for "Red Rose," he called Qayah. And she'd blush, and her cheeks would become so red that even her red curls would start feeling jealous.

Skyurr, Armenian for "Squirrel," she nicknamed him, because of his chestnut hair.

They would clandestinely meet every night at the small cottage she had rented after the old house got burned to the ground. The cottage was also her workshop; a very busy one, as she had become the quarter's only skilled seamstress after Vartouhi's death. Avi would come after dark and sneak in from the back window that she'd leave open for him. Every night they would laugh. They would weep. They would trade small stories and big secrets. She didn't hide anything from him. The night she told him about Marine and Aslan, they cried in each other's arms until dawn.

They would also play house. She'd make him try on the dresses she was sewing. He'd make her kiss him in return. She'd teach him Armenian. He'd teach her Hebrew.

"Parev."[7]

"Ma Shlomesh?"[8]

"Yess kezi gesirem."[9]

Nothing sexual ever happened, or even almost happened between them. As if they were beyond the flesh. An eighteen-year-old baby girl and a nineteen-year-old baby boy: Two kids trapped in a spider web that they couldn't see.

Not just yet.

Negan's father Shafik, who had become Qayah's un-official guardian after Vartouhi's passing, had asked her repeatedly to move in with them. But she constantly refused, despite Negan's supplications.

"Thank you so much Ammo, but I prefer to stay here. I wouldn't want to disturb you with all the clients who keep coming and going. Besides, you're just three steps away from me anyway. It's practically as if I were living with you."

Negan didn't understand.

"But Qayah, we'd become real sisters! You could sleep in my room!"

She didn't know the real reason that was holding her friend back and she was upset. Qayah didn't dare tell her at first. Would she also think that Avi was evil? Would she

....

7   Armenian for "hello."

8   Hebrew for "how are you?"

9   Armenian for "I love you."

stop being her friend? But one month into the relationship, on a cold January morning, Qayah gathered her courage and blurted it all out to her.

"This is the best day of my life," Negan exclaimed. "Your happiness is and will always be the source of mine."

That was it. No judgments made. No explanations needed. True, pure friendship.

It lasted till autumn, her parenthesis of bliss. Ten months of cheating her grief and loneliness. Ten months of forgetting that torment will always come back to bite her; that as long as she had to invent hope, it will never exist.

One October evening Shafik came to check on her unexpectedly. He never came in the evenings. Since she wasn't coming to the door, he got concerned and forced it open. He found them sound asleep in the back bedroom, nestled in each other's arms. They hadn't heard the knocks. They were hugging face to face, glued together like a big swan's wings. Qayah was the left, and Avi the right.

Shafik took one look at Avi, and knew who he was. *What* he was. His rage was palpable, but he didn't make a scene. Nor did he say one word to Qayah. He went back to the living room/workspace, opened the cottage's door, waited for the young man to step outside, and followed him, closing the door behind them,

They stayed there for five minutes talking. Shafik did all the talking, Avi just listened. Then Avi walked away, and Qayah was not to see him again for eighteen years. As if he had vanished.

She kept expecting to see him, though. For eighteen interminable years, she did. Expectation—the harshest of all methods of self-persecution.

The next morning, a calm Shafik knocked again on her door. Negan had spent the night with Qayah, trying to console what was left of her. Shafik wasn't alone; there was a tall, robust man with him. He looked rather old.

"This is the man you are going to marry," Shafik informed her.

And that was it.

She was now engaged to a man she didn't know. A man she couldn't help but detest on sight. A man who would "save her from scandal."

His name was Bassem.

—

Jerusalem—Sunday, October 5, 1930

So many people talk about freedom. "We want freedom." "We will fight for our freedom." "Freedom is everything."

Freedom is a ridiculous impossibility. That's what it is. Just like choice. We are born into a cage we haven't picked, at a time we had no say in deciding, in a place we previously knew nothing about, having features we did not shape, and ethnicities and religions and character traits we did not choose.

Some of us are dealt bad cards; others are dealt good ones, sometimes even great ones.

It is called cynicism, and it's a divine trait. Humans have always designed their gods as cynical. An astute form of self-consolation.

Ammo Shafik told us a story once about a faraway land where people are always happy. No one is ever poor, or hungry, or homeless there. They all have nice clothes, many toys, loving parents, easy jobs. He said that these people would sometimes kill themselves because of how happy they are. They are happy to the point of desperation. When I heard the story, I felt so angry at them.

But then I thought: Maybe those people were cunning enough to leave before life went downhill. What a magnificent slap in the face of the cynical card dealer.

♦ ♡ ♤ ♧

Downhill.
Life unmistakably goes there.

⌐

Bassem would sometimes take her with him on his short trips, whenever he didn't have long hours of hard work ahead, especially after he had stopped mining and had became a truck driver. She was tremendously relieved that he had changed jobs. Every time he used to go into one of the limestone mines of Deir Yassin, a small Palestinian village on the outskirts of Jerusalem, Qayah feared he wouldn't come out again. And after years of ineffective searches, someone would eventually find his scattered bones and bring them back to her in a shoe box. Many nights she'd wake up screaming, imagining there was a skeleton by her side. And no matter how hard Bassem tried to reassure her, the tenacious anxiety wouldn't go away. She would lie for hours staring in the dark, too scared to go back to sleep. Only when he announced to her that one of the town's well-off inhabitants had offered him a job as a truck driver, did the panic and insomnia gradually disappear.

Deir Yassin was built on the slopes of a hill, about eight hundred meters above sea level. The city center of Jerusalem was less than five kilometers away to the east. The village was separated from the city by a valley planted with fig trees and olive orchards. Qayah loved the carriage ride to the stone crushers where Bassem worked. It made her feel peaceful and light, as if she was shedding away her burdens on the road. She also loved Deir Yassin. It reminded her of home village of Aintab.

"Why don't we move here?" she asked him more than once.

She couldn't stand living under the same roof with her mother-in-law anymore. Ah, to be away, even if only five kilometers away, from that perfidious woman! To be away from the probability of Avi too, and the stinging she still felt in her gut every time she went out of the house and expected to run into him. She would miss Negan terribly, of course, but her friend could always come visit her, and even stay with them for as long as she wanted. After all, she was still unmarried, still waiting for love, that crazy romantic girl, not disheartened by the categorical *no* of the age of thirty-three.

But Bassem would always object.

"Deir Yassin is an all-Muslim village, Qayah!"

"So what? You have many Muslim friends and everyone likes you here. I am sure they would welcome us with open arms."

Bassem was well aware of the animosity between his mother and his wife. They both had extremely strong characters, too strong to even try to hide their mutual aversion from him. Every time Qayah suggested the idea of moving out, he'd lovingly pinch her cheek and end the conversation, promising, "I'll think about it." But she didn't believe him. Even he did not believe himself. He didn't feel capable of doing this to his mother, Fadwa. He knew how attached she was to him.

The Barakats had a small herd of goats, which Bassem's youngest brother tended. Qayah often lent a helping hand when he needed to milk the females. But Bassem wouldn't let her work after their marriage ("People would think I am unable to provide for you"), and she missed creating and sewing clothes. Most of all, she missed feeling productive—or at least useful.

One of the goats was remarkably ugly and obnoxious, and Qayah had secretly named her Fadwa. Negan's stepmother was also called Fadwa, so the goat became the subject of countless inside jokes between the two friends.

"I squeezed Fadwa's teats today!"

♦ ♡ ♤ ♧

"Whose? The goat's or your mother-in-law's?"

"Have you noticed how Fadwa's beard has grown?"

"Whose? The goat's or your stepmother's?"

It was a never-ending game, a Souk Okaz[10] for puns. Who will crack the funniest one today? Each one-liner would instigate the next, and the two young women would go on bantering and giggling until they felt avenged enough for the day.

One late spring morning, as she was sitting next to Bassem on their way to Deir Yassin, Qayah was remembering the previous day's events and smiling. Fadwa (the mother-in-law, not the stepmother or the goat) almost caught them in full display of their comical talents.

"What are you chuckling so hard about? You sound like two crazy hens," she said hostilely.

Negan started mumbling something, but Qayah stopped her. She just stood there with an expression like ice, and looked her mother-in-law straight in the eyes without blinking. Fadwa hesitated for a few seconds, then she left the patio. Qayah turned to Negan and calmly said:

"I pulled out Fadwa's horns today."

Negan almost fell on her back from laughing.

Once they got to Deir Yassin, Qayah sat in the shade of a cherry tree, near a well that looked a lot like her late grandmother's, waiting for Bassem to finish his half a shift on that day. An old woman that seemed to appear from nowhere suddenly approached her. She'd never seen her around there before, even though many of the village's faces had become familiar to her.

"Aren't you the Girl with Two Names?" the woman asked her abruptly.

She was referring to Qayah's nickname in the Christian Quarter of Jerusalem. That was how she had come to be

....

10   Ancient Arabia's bustling market.

known after the famous incident at the wedding. Her second nickname was "the Seamstress' Daughter." Neither bothered her. The first reminded her of how she stood up to Fadwa, and the second, of both her seamstress mothers.

Qayah was intrigued though. How did that woman recognize her? *It must be the red hair*, she thought. During all those years in Jerusalem, she had never met anyone, male or female, who had the same hair color. *Al-Saherah*, "the Witch," was in fact her third nickname, one she wasn't aware of. People only called her that behind her back. No one ever dared say it to her face.

"Yes," Qayah answered.

"You will soon bear a daughter," said the old woman.

Qayah jumped, startled. Her heart skipped a beat.

After thirteen years of childless marriage, she and Bassem had given up the idea of ever having kids. She didn't want kids, anyway. It had taken Bassem six months of preliminaries, and relentless persuasion, to be able to make love to her. She was incapable of conceiving the idea of giving birth to a baby from "down there." A psychological block had transformed into a physical inability. But she couldn't help but feel sorry for her husband. He has been so patient and tolerant with her. And even though he never said anything, and never blamed her, she knew in her heart that he badly wanted a child.

"Who are you?" Qayah asked.

The woman, whose face was severely wrinkled, ignored the question and repeated the same words, in the same exact tone, like a machine.

"You will soon have a daughter." Then she added, "But you have to swear something."

"What?"

"You must call her Fatima."

Qayah stood there, speechless.

♦ ♡ ♤ ♧

"Swear," the old woman insisted.

"I swear."

⤙

Deir Yassin—Thursday, May 17, 1945

I had another nightmare yesterday. I know this nightmare very well. I used to have it a lot as a child. But this time, it was the red-haired boy who was choking me with his hands, and Mother was applauding him.

Could Death be another beginning? I hope not. I am tired and I need a conclusive end.

I am tired and drained and spent. But most of all, I am afraid.

Hush little baby don't you cry,

Mama's gonna sing you a lullaby.

⤙

"*Finally!*" said Bassem's mother Fadwa, when he proudly gave her the news of Qayah's pregnancy. "It is about time she gave you a son," she added resentfully. "I just pray that the baby will be fine with such an old womb carrying it."

"Qayah is not old, mother! She's barely thirty-three. You had my sister Hania when you were forty-nine!"

That caught her off guard. Nonetheless, it was true. She did have her youngest daughter when she was forty-nine, almost exactly twenty-four years ago. She had bragged about that repeatedly to showcase her outstanding fertility. Fertility was how a woman's worth was calculated. That, and her ability to keep her husband satisfied and content.

Fadwa had gotten married rather late. She was already twenty-one and bordering on spinsterhood by those days' standards. She wanted to make it up to her husband and get back at all those who had considered her no longer marriageable. Her first child, Bassem, was born in 1894, exactly nine months after her wedding, and her last, Hania, in 1921. In the twenty-seven years between the two, she gave birth to four more daughters, two of whom died soon after birth, and four more sons. Ten children in all. She was very proud.

Bassem was the last of his brothers to have gotten married, although he was the eldest. He was thirty-eight on his wedding day, eighteen years older than his bride. When his friend Shafik told him he had found the perfect girl for him, he was reluctant at first. But the minute he laid eyes on Qayah, it was love at first sight. He only worried about the age difference between them.

"It's better this way," Shafik told him. "She has many years ahead of her to give you plenty of healthy, strong sons."

As it turned out, she gave him none.

Bassem's mother and Qayah couldn't stand each other, and navigating between them hasn't been easy, to say the least, especially since they all lived under the same roof in the family's old house. Tradition dictated that the firstborn son was the one entitled to his parents' house, provided they live with him and he looks after them. Qayah had trouble getting pregnant, which made her an even easier target for Fadwa. In turn, Qayah didn't spare the old woman and never missed a chance to infuriate her. And she knew how. Over the years, she became an expert in pushing her mother-in-law's buttons without any effort. But Bassem loved them both dearly, and he was wise enough not to succumb to their respective attempts at emotional blackmail in the war over him.

Fadwa mumbled some unintelligible words and went on with kneading the dough for the weekly bread bake. She had three living daughters and five daughters-in-law, but she never allowed any of them to participate in the sacred ritual. She didn't trust any of them enough, especially not "*Hal Armaniyeh,* 'that Armenian,'" which was how she disdainfully referred to Qayah behind her back.

"What will you call the boy? He should carry your father's name, *Allah Yerhamo.*"[11]

"We already have four Faraj in the family, *Oum* Bassem! All my brothers have granted you this wish. Plus, we don't know yet if it's going to be a boy."

"My wish? How can you say that? *Ya aayb el shoom!*"[12] It is not a wish; it is a sacred custom. And you are the eldest son after all! But you are right. I doubt she's capable of bearing boys anyway. I still can't understand why, out of all the good Palestinian girls there are around, Shafik chose that Armenian to be your wife. He clearly has a weak spot for Armenians, that man!"

"When will you stop calling her 'that Armenian'? Haven't you had enough of this consuming hatred already?"

Bassem was starting to get really exasperated, but Fadwa was canny and manipulative enough to indulge his mood so as not to alienate him.

"Well, she never answers when I call her Qamar," she replied in a conciliatory voice.

"It's because her name is Qayah—not Qamar!"

"But you told me it was the same…"

"No, Mother, it is not the same at all!"

"Never mind *ya oyouni*, my eyes!"[13] she said affectionately. This is a glorious day and we should celebrate! I am seventy-three, with one foot already in the grave. But I will get to hold my eldest son's baby in my arms before I die. What's not to celebrate? How about I prepare you a *Mansaf*?"[14]

....

11 Arabic for "God rest his soul."

12 Arabic slang for "shame on you."

13 Arabic for "my eyes," a form of expressing fondness.

14 A traditional Arabic dish made of lamb served with rice or bulgur.

She knew that it was his favorite dish, and thought that she could always win him over with food, convinced as she was that Qayah couldn't even fry an egg. She also knew how to use her old age to draw his pity.

"It is indeed a glorious day!" the fifty-one-year-old said smiling. "I am going to be a father! I hope it will be a girl. I'll call her Qana[15]…" "Oh and one more thing," Bassem added. "Qayah and I are moving to Deir Yassin."

He stood up and left the room, leaving his mother thunderstruck.

‌⁀

Jerusalem—Saturday, September 6, 1945

Hush little baby, don't say a word,
  Mama's gonna buy you a shiny sword.
In my sleep, I keep seeing wild horses running in an endless field. The field has no beginning and no end, and the horses are galloping nonstop. Suddenly the field becomes a daunting desert, and all the horses stop running at once. They bump into each other and fall to the sandy ground. Then little by little, one after the other, they grow wings and start flying away, into the distant horizon.

No shoes would survive this journey. Can cobblers mend feet, too? They should. Whenever I see a shoeshine polishing someone's shoes, I remember my father. I remember Jesus bending over his disciples' feet, washing them meticulously. I remember all the human weeping willows. People who need to bend in order to do their jobs

....

15   *Qana Al-Jalil*, also spelled Cana, a town in Galilee. According to the Fourth Gospel, Jesus performed his first public miracle there, the turning of a large quantity of water into wine at a wedding feast. It is of major significance to Eastern Christians. There is speculation about the exact location of Qana. Some scholars assert that it is the village with the same name located in Southern Lebanon. Others claim that it refers to the town of Kafr Kanna, about 7 kilometers northeast of Nazareth, in Palestine.

are the nameless kings and queens of this Earth.

Colors aren't real. The white milk I drank from my mother's breasts was black. The red blood flowing in my veins is black.

Mayrik, where are you? I don't want to be a boot anymore when I grow up.

I just want to be a soothing balm on your wounded feet.

⌐

When Qayah discovered she was pregnant, only a few months after her strange encounter with the prophetic old woman, and she told Bassem the whole story, he laughed at her.

"Come on! She's surely an impostor! It is a mere coincidence. If the baby is a girl, I want to call her *Qana!*"

He refused to discuss the matter any further and she didn't insist. She was ecstatic that he had finally agreed to move to Deir Yassin, a decision he clearly made under the influence of the adrenaline rush he experienced when she told him he was going to be a father. She knew that it was his way of rewarding her, and she didn't want to oppose him for fear he'd change his mind.

But soon after Qana was born, the infant got sick. Not quite sick, but she would cry for hours for no reason. They took her to three different doctors, but none of them seemed to understand what was wrong with her. Her body seemed to function normally, and there were no signs of an illness or an infection.

Fadwa blamed Qayah.

"God is punishing you because you forced my son to move out of Jerusalem and live with Muslims."

Qayah, on the other hand, blamed Bassem. At first he ignored his wife's accusations, but after three months of sleepless nights with a constant crying that nothing seemed to appease, he gave in.

"Look, if we ever have a second daughter, we will call her Fatima. I promise, *Aala sharafi*, on my honor." And just as soon as Bassem uttered those words, Qana's fits started to diminish, until they stopped completely. Less than two years later, in March 1948, Qayah found out she was pregnant again.

↩

The Israeli-Arab war didn't just drop in on them. They were expecting it, hearing its growls and smelling its stench long before it broke out.

Right after the Deir Yassin massacre on April 9, 1948, and the battle for Jerusalem that followed, where so many of his family members and friends lost their lives, Bassem decided to escape with his pregnant wife and little daughter, leaving the whole country altogether, not foreseeing any possible end to the conflict.

They packed what they could of their lives and left on the 23rd of May 1948. But not before Qayah had gotten the news that Avi had been killed the day before. He was visiting a relative who was originally from Germany. Avi—Aaron Goldberg—was one of the lucky few who survived the horrors of the Holocaust and made it to the Ramat Rachel kibbutz south of Jerusalem three years earlier. It was the day when the Arab forces attacked the settlement; 31 Jordanians, and 13 Israelis, died, and Avi was one of the casualties.

He had categorically refused to carry a weapon, not even to defend himself. He was shot while helping the injured on both sides. One eye witness affirmed that it was Avi's own brother who killed him. Haim was a ruthless and hardline Zionist who never forgave Avi for sympathizing with the Palestinians and not fighting for Israel. Qayah's friend Negan had died too, only a few days before Avi, hit by a traitorous sniper bullet during the heavy house-to-house fighting between the Arab legion

and the Israeli forces in the Arab neighborhood of Jerusalem.

Two more drawers in the morgue, two more sorrows to carefully fold in Qayah's luggage.

Deir Yassin—Sunday, May 23, 1948

Between me and myself there's a tomb so inviting that I don't know how long I can resist its call.

What's the purpose of all this? Is there even a purpose? Which is worse, the lack of a purpose or its existence? Which is more wicked: science or religion?

Do the questions ever cease? Or do the dead keep wondering what happened to those they had left behind?

Goodbye, Negan. Goodbye, Avi.

They first settled in Marwahin, a small village in the South of Lebanon at the border with Palestine, where Qayah gave birth to their second daughter. Bassem kept his word and registered her as Fatima at the local records office. Fadwa wasn't there to protest the Muslim name. She had decided to put her second foot in the grave at the age of seventy-five and had passed away in her sleep before the start of the war. "It was about time," was Qayah's only reaction, when the distraught Bassem gave her the news. He never forgave her for that.

Even so, they enjoyed six years of relative serenity in Marwahin. Bassem helped the tobacco farmers in grow and harvest, and Qayah gradually returned to her previous days of sewing glory. But they had to move again after Fatima's tragic death, which made life in Marwahin unbearable for them, especially for Qayah.

It was on the 3rd of September, in 1954, Fatima's sixth birthday. Qayah had just finished baking the cake, and she left her two girls alone in the house to pay a quick visit to a sick neighbor. When she came back, Fatima was complaining of abdominal pains. It took Bassem four days to finally find someone to help him get her to the nearest hospital, which was two and half hours away by car. But it was too late. The little girl died on the road. After having performed an autopsy on her, the doctor told them that a needle had migrated to her heart and caused her a cardiac tamponade, which led to her death. Qayah had forgotten her sewing case unattended when she had left the house.

"This is my punishment," Qayah thought.

She was five months' pregnant at the time. Again, the pregnancy had been a shock to both of them, as she was forty-two and Bassem sixty. They left Marwahin exactly one week after the funeral, and Qayah gave birth to their third daughter on Christmas Eve in Beirut. It was a complicated delivery, and Qayah nearly lost her life during labor. Bassem named the baby girl *Najat*, savior, since he perceived her as salvation to his recently bereaved family.

But salvation was a station that Qayah had long since passed on the train ride of horrors that was her life.

⚬

Marwahin—Friday, September 3, 1954.

Does anyone else on the face of this Earth know how much it aches to sense time and space by the stream of loved ones we have lost?

There are so many bodies scattered behind me, buried or abandoned or forsaken, in so many different places, that I can no longer keep track of them. This world has become just one big graveyard.

Tell me, God, how many times is one person allowed to say,

♦ ♡ ♤ ♧

"Forgive me for having outlived you?"
  Goodbye, Fatima.

⤙

Bassem managed to rent a cheap apartment in a shabby building in Bourj Hammoud, Beirut's Armenian quarter. It wasn't easy to find, but his wife Qayah was an Armenian, and Armenians helped each other and stuck together. Bassem began mending shoes for a living. Whenever Qayah brought him lunch at the tiny shop he had rented around the corner, and saw him bending over a pair of shoes, Qayah would remember her father Nazar and the time they were all living happily in Aintab. *I wonder if his knees are still bleeding*, she thought.

But Bassem's income barely covered the rent for the apartment and shop, and the couple had two mouths to feed. So Qayah started cleaning houses. That's how she managed to enroll Qana in the quarter's Armenian elementary school. Her eldest daughter Qana could study there for free, in exchange for Qayah cleaning the classrooms.

As for Najat, she was sick, "sick in the head," as Qayah's neighbors whispered. Qayah first discovered her condition when the girl turned five. She had taken her to the Armenian School and enrolled her there, just like her sister Qana before her. One month later, in January 1960, the head teacher summoned her. He told her that Najat had problems, *"Aysdegh,* here."[16] he said, pointing to the child's brain.

"We tried," he added, "but your daughter is unresponsive. Either she sits in class doing nothing, like a sleepwalker, or she gets totally frantic. You should take her to a doctor."

Qayah had already noticed that Najat had fits and temper swings, but she wasn't knowledgeable enough to suspect that

....

16   Armenian for "here."

there was something wrong with her. The girl could speak and walk, and she showed no evident signs of sickness. Qayah used to think that her youngest was just a moody child, until the head teacher gave her his awful verdict: "She's retarded."

But Najat's problem wasn't developmental. It was hormonal and chemical.

A doctor? They couldn't afford one. So Qayah went to an apothecary and explained the situation. The pharmacist reached up to one of the shelves and selected a box.

"This," he said confidently. "Just keep giving her this and she'll be fine. One tablet every morning. We will increase the dosage gradually."

The box read: Veronal.

It should have read: "Najat's death sentence."

⟶

Bourj Hammoud—Sunday, July 19, 1964

Scrub, Qayah, Scrub. This is your day off, the day when you should be cleaning your own house instead of other people's houses.

But it's useless. No matter how hard I brush the floor, how well I wash the plates, how meticulously I sponge the bathroom and dust the shelves, everything remains dirty. I see black stains everywhere, on the walls, on the bed sheets, on the curtains, on my clothes.

Could I be the dirt?

Could it be that I should wipe myself out?

⟶

When her health started to waning at the age of fifty-eight, Qayah had to stop cleaning houses and go back to sewing clothes, despite her vow after Fatima's death never to touch a needle again. But she was too poor to keep vows. She couldn't afford to stop working. Her husband had become a street vendor because he could no longer cover the cobbling shop's rent, and her daughter Najat needed constant medication.

It was in 1970, that when Bassem finally decided to get himself and his wife Lebanese identity cards. He could have applied for them any time since 1958, but he kept procrastinating, feeling it would be a treason to his beloved Palestine. Eventually he had to give in, because he was told he could become entitled to Lebanese healthcare if he did. Their eldest daughter Qana had gained nationality when she married a Lebanese one year earlier. Their youngest, Najat, already had it, having been born in Lebanon, just like her late sister Fatima, who had been not only born on, but buried in, Lebanese soil.

Qayah became apprehensive when her husband hid the documents. She eventually found them tucked inside one of his socks and showed them to Qana. When her bewildered daughter told her that she was registered as Qamar Sarraf, Qayah lost her mind. Bassem pretended it wasn't his fault, that it was the clerk who did that for some reason and that he, Bassem, didn't find out until it was too late. He was clearly lying. How would a clerk know that the name Qayah could be interchangeable with Qamar? She was sure it was something he did on purpose, to grant his deceased mother her long lasting wish.

To punish him, she overcame her obsession with cleanness and promised a bunch of kids a piece of candy in exchange for every mouse they'd kill and bring her back. She started planting dead mice in their small apartment in the most improbable places—under Bassem's folded underwear, inside one of his slippers, on top of the closet where he kept his hat... Her husband was a robust man, but he was inexplicably terrified of mice. Whenever he saw one, he would start squawking like a seagull.

Following seven days of horror, on the last of which she had put a mouse under his pillow and he almost had a stroke discovering it, she decided it was enough. He had served his sentence. Qayah knew that Bassem had never stopped feeling guilty toward Fadwa ever since they moved out and went to live on their own in Deir Yassin. His mother had fallen seriously sick soon afterward, and in his mind, there was a definite link between the two events.

"I hope that evil witch is rotting in hell."

Do sons ever outgrow their mothers? Us women keep blaming men for our misfortune, for the injustices we are subjected to, but those men are first and foremost our sons. Sons of women who adore them. Women who treat them like royalty. Women who put them first. Women who forgive them everything. Women who tell them "yes" after "yes." Women who keep wishing to swallow them back into their viscera so that they could fill the unfillable void they had left behind. At the moment of birth, mothers get rid of the daughters, while they give up the sons despite themselves, forced only by the laws of biology.

Inside every man making love to a woman, there's a small boy trying to sneak back into his mother's womb.

⸺

Beirut—Tuesday, November 10, 1970

Poverty is a soul breaker.
Poverty is a soul breaker.
POVERTY IS A SOUL BREAKER.

⸺

"I see pink. I see pink"

She couldn't take it anymore.

She had made up her mind a long time ago anyway. She was just waiting for the bait on the hook to become irresistible.

♦ ♡ ♤ ♧

Today felt perfect: She had awakened mouthwatering for death.

It was her birthday after all. The ideal day to die.

Soon Najat would wake up, and Qana would arrive for her daily early afternoon visit. "I must be quick," she thought. Yesterday Qana told her that a man had thrown himself off the roof of the five-story building where she lived with her husband and daughter. Qayah couldn't imagine herself doing that. Staining the street underneath with blood and crushed bones and naked flesh! She needed a clean, discrete death. One that wouldn't embarrass her family.

She sat down for a minute, out of breath like she'd often been lately. A bee was stuck on the cover of the jam jar on the kitchen table. *The cover must be sticky. I should clean it.* Then she shrugged. *Later, later.*

The bee was flapping its minuscule wings and producing a nervous humming sound. She didn't feel any pity for it. We're all trapped. Stop complaining.

Qayah went to check on Najat in the bedroom. She was still asleep, lying on her back, as still as a cadaver, her dense unctuous hair covering her face. Qayah cautiously drew her ear near her daughter's mouth to make sure she was still breathing. *Those pills are killing her slowly.* Najat had blue-black hair, the same as her sister's Qana. *Just like their Aunt Hosanna,* Qayah thought, and one more wall in her glass heart cracked. None of her daughters had inherited her red locks. Fatima's hair was chestnut brown. *My sweet Fatima,* she remembered, and the memory blew out the last dithering candle in her soul. *Was I wrong to tell Qana?* she wondered.

It didn't matter anymore. What's done is done. She had felt that her daughter deserved to know. Qana has asked her so many questions in the past, questions that she's never answered. Now she has answered everything. Even what hasn't been asked.

Just don't tell your father about Avi. He doesn't deserve to be hurt.

She went back to the kitchen and headed to the cabinet under the sink, where she kept all the cleaning products. She slowly opened the cabinet's door with her now constantly trembling hands. Then she squatted and reached for a container behind the detergent bottle.

The container was bright yellow with black scribblings on it.

It read: "RAT POISON."

"DANGER."

"DO NOT TAKE INTERNALLY."

But Qayah couldn't read.

She looked at the sticker with the skull and crossbones.

That's when she saw them. They were all there, their faces on the box, smiling and waving to her: Nazar, Hagop, Hosanna, Marine, Grigor, Vartouhi, Negan, Fatima…

And Avi.

I already died for good the first time I lost you. All the deaths I've lived through before were just rehearsals. All the ones after were unnecessary validations.

I am the sixty-six-year-old overdue corpse of a lifeless eighteen-year-old-girl.

She swallowed the gray crystals and crossed to the other side.

Beirut—Tuesday, April 11, 1978

I finally know what dead means, Mayrik.

I am not afraid anymore.

Goodbye, Qayah.

[2]

QADAR

(Beirut, 1970 –)

Granddaughter of Qayah
Mother of Qamar
Daughter of Qana

"She whose eyes awaken thunder"

♛

T he **Queen of Hearts** is a nonconformist and an adventurer who is forever curious about life. She needs variety and change, and gives ample time and energy to exploring all possibilities. She is empathetic and sensual, and has an inflated expectation of perfect love.
Her destiny is ruled by the **Emotions**.

The morning after my death
we will sit in cafés
but I will not be there.
I will not be.
—ETEL ADNAN
Lebanese poetess

He opened the door hastily. Slammed it back shut.

She jumped, startled.

Quick. Quick. Threw the book away. Gasped for breath. Tried to put some order into her untamable mane.

He walked in. Didn't say a word. Didn't even glance at her. Sat on the chair facing hers. Grabbed her arm. Drew her brutally toward him. Sat her on his lap. Pulled her hair. Sucked her neck. Bit her lower lip.

She screamed: "Ouch!" Ferociously scratched his back. Bit him back in his upper lip. Inhaled the dizzying smell of his desire. Took him inside her slowly, without any preliminaries. Thought: *I am the worst.* Felt: Wow! Uttered: "Ummm…"

How did it happen so fast? This takeover, this "invasion," as she perceived it. As she *lived* it. How can it be possible? Less than a week ago, he, *this*, did not exist. And now he, *this*, occupied all the space inside and around her. It had been the swiftest surrender of history. She didn't even put up a fight.

Like most children of wars, her vocabulary and her vision of the world were largely influenced by terms of warfare: "invade," "occupy," "surrender."

But most of all, "fight."

It all started on March 14th of 2005. *Qadar*, Arabic for destiny, was waving the Lebanese flag and screaming her lungs out with the massive crowd in downtown Beirut, when suddenly she felt a gentle but firm hand from behind pick up her falling black bra strap and put it back into place on her shoulder. That's when she looked back, and saw him for the first time. He said nothing. He just smiled then disappeared in the multitude.

That same evening, when the huge demonstration was over, she went to have a drink with a group of her friends in one of *Monnot Street's* numerous pubs. Scotch on the rocks. That was her poison. "Wine is for women," she always said with a revolted frown. She was feminine in many ways—at least according to the common clichés that dictated what feminine was and was not. But something in her rebelled against monochromatic textures and longed for the nuances of androgyny: what she considered to be the perfect human being. She felt ecstatic when a Brazilian regression therapist she had met once on a plane told her, just by holding her hand for five awkward minutes: "You've had numerous past lives in which you've been a man." She didn't really believe that sort of shit, but she still loved how what he said sustained her personal mythology: the fantasy that she was one of those who represented the duality, male and female, each in its right, strongest manifestation.

Everyone in the place was already drunk from the excitement of the "Cedar Revolution." A formidable wave of change had hit Lebanon following the assassination of Prime Minister Rafik Hariri on the 14th of February. "Enough with the blood shedding! Enough with the divisions! We love life and we want to live it, not merely survive it."

Also: "Syrians, out!"

People had woken up. Finally.

Or had they?

And there he was again, standing in a back corner of the same pub, gazing at her insistently via the mirror that faced the bar where she was sitting. As soon as their eyes, met he stood up and walked toward her. She appreciated this urgency, this getting-into-action carpe diem style. She loathed the men she called the "mollusks," who would just spend the whole evening glancing then shying away, staring at women back and forth, lacking the guts to leap into fire. She's never been attracted to those who let themselves be devoured. She needed a predator. Someone who could be her match. And there he was, right before her eyes, indulging himself in the pre-banquet phase. This time, he spoke.

No pathetic pickup lines, no pointless preliminaries. No "what's your name" and "what do you do in life."

"Have you ever read Sandra Cisneros?"

If there was one way to immediately catch her attention, that was it.

"No. Should I?"

"She's a black lace bra
kind of woman, the kind who serves
up suicide with every kamikaze
poured in the neon blue of evening."

He recited the verses with an almost flawless English accent, and without emphasis. She couldn't stand people who declaimed poetry as if they were Moses on Mount Sinai.

"Did you just Google that or are you in the habit of learning poems about bras by heart?"

"Only those that mention my favorite color of bra."

"How refreshing! A man obsessed by the color rather than the size."

He laughed. He had a wet laugh, one that could irrigate deserts and turn them into the greenest of forests.

Deserts just like her heart.

He also had fine-looking hands. With graceful fingers and neat nails. That was the first thing she noticed in a man. That, and his teeth. His were strikingly white, perfectly aligned between two plump lips. Not too plump. Just plump enough.

"What happened today was superb, but it'll go nowhere. Another dead end. I hope I'll be proven wrong, but I have no more faith in our people."

She thought so too. She had been disappointed by the Lebanese, especially the politicians, too many times to indulge herself in the luxury of optimism. But she was trying to maintain a positive attitude anyway. To consider this could actually be a fresh start for her martyrized country. She had to.

After an hour of stimulating exchanges about how dangerous *Hezbollah*[17] was, how poetry would never die, and how sexy a loose bra strap can be, he said out of the blue:

"I have an erection."

She wasn't the least scandalized. Nor certainly offended.

"I have an erection too," she replied simply.

"I can see that. There's a bump growing on your forehead," he joked.

It didn't occur to him to ask her: "How could you have an erection? You're a woman." He didn't even think it. He had immediately understood what she meant: That she was a sapiosexual, one who was attracted to and aroused by intelligence. Her clitoris, and the rest of her sexual equipment, were located in her brain. That is why so very few men had been
....

17   Literally The Party of God, a Shia Islamist militant group.

◇ ♥ ♤ ♧

able to find her G-spot. "To me, G stands for Gray matter," she'd once told a pedant British sexologist who was trying to impress her with his knowledge of female physiology.

Omar already intuited that about her. Not to mention that he had come up with a double-edged compliment: he was flattering himself as much as he was flattering her. Arrogant but cunning. That could very well be the exact moment when—and the first reason why—Qadar fell in love with him. Only a couple of hours later, she was already lying in a messy bed in a messy room in his messy apartment in *Hamra* district.[18] Her best friend Nina frowned disapprovingly when she told her she was leaving the pub with him.

Nina was in fact "Nazla." She was named after her paternal grandmother, and she absolutely abhorred her outmoded name. "I don't think it was ever fashionable. Not even B.C.," Qadar would naughtily say every time Nina complained to her about how unfashionable "Nazla" was.

Primary school had been a constant agony for the little girl, as the kids made fun of her on a daily basis. *Nazla El Habla. Nazla El Bassla. Nazla Tala'a.*[19] The nasty nicknames wouldn't stop rolling. All her classmates teased her but one: Qadar. To Nazla's good fortune, Qadar was that one girl you wouldn't want to mess with. Beginning of fourth grade, she took Nazla under her wing. They became inseparable ever since.

First day of middle school, Nazla decided that from that moment on, she would become Nina. Her father had gifted her mother a bottle of perfume for her birthday a few weeks earlier. It was called *"L'Air Du Temps"* by Nina Ricci, and the ten-year-old girl loved both the fragrance and the sound of the name. In solidarity with her friend, Qadar converted into Dina.

....

18 A major commercial street in Beirut.
19 Arabic for The Stupid, The Onion, The Uphill, all rhyming with Nazla.

Nina and Dina were an indestructible unit. The first was the quiet and conformist one, the second the crazy and rebellious one. It takes both kinds to build a solid, long-lasting friendship.

"Dina! You just met the guy! Now he's going to think you're easy!"

Qadar let out an irritated sigh. She never understood, nor submitted, to the patriarchal logic that divided women into two categories: "easy" and "hard-to-get." She saw it differently: She was either interested in a man, or not. She had no patience whatsoever for game playing. If the man felt the need to "beg for it" in order to appreciate her company, then he wasn't her type. Thus, "to hell with him." It was as simple as that.

"To me, he's the one being easy. I think of myself as the hunter, Nina. Remember?"

"But what about Fouad?"

Qadar walked away. This was not the time nor the place for that question.

The more she got to know Omar in the following days, the more she not only fell more passionately for him, but also *liked* him. She was one of those adventurous hara-kiri kind of people who are quick to use the word "love." Too quick. Maybe it was because it scared the hell out of her that she used it so lightly: to dedramatize it.

"Love" for Qadar almost always came before "like." First, the intellectual and physical jolt, then the ethical evaluation of the person. First the Homo Sapiens and Homo Sensualis, then the Homo Moralis. She knew that one can be attracted to someone's mind and body, only to discover later they are a prick on the human level. Smart people weren't necessarily nice or honest.

Wittiness encourages deceit. Those who were both clever *and* decent deserved a medal in this Machiavellian world. At least she thought so.

◇ ♥ ♤ ♧

Qadar liked Omar for many reasons. Not only was he an intelligent and kindhearted man wrapped up in a strong personality with uncompromising dispositions (the perfect combination in her opinion), but he was also a wild hedonist who loathed sugary words, actions, and emotions in bed. Pleasure came through unbridled savagery, not sweet romance. Camille Saint-Saens' *Carnival of the Animals* rather than Chopin's *Nocturno*. Also, he had the right amount of cynicism in him: not too much so as to be insufferable, not too little so as to sound naïve. He stood in the middle between innocence and decadence, the fabulous amalgam of an adorable boy and a raging demon.

She had to admit to herself that she also liked him because of his name and the religion that came with it. Despite all the talk about a so-called coexistence, a Christian woman falling for a Muslim man, or vice versa, was still taboo in Lebanon (Will it ever cease to be, excluding a few transgressions here and there, too few to be considered a tangible progress?). Qadar loved to break taboos, especially by accident. She'd seldom been a *provocateur* on purpose. But whenever she unintentionally challenged the system, simply because of who she was and how she lived, she enjoyed it immensely. It was like a bonus for her. An added value to being true to herself.

Also, he didn't give a damn about religion. Just like her. "I don't like to waste my time with hypothesizes. And I'm too spontaneous to ever follow a script."

She discovered that Omar still had first times to give, amazingly for a man in his mid-forties. And she liked that about him, too. She never liked being just the repetition of someone. Of something. At best, a premiere after a chain of rehearsals. A sexual and sentimental "déjà-vu." It was unavoidable of course, but she preferred someone who would be able to say, after they did something, anything together: "This is the first time I've ever done that." This, her forty-five-year-old lover was surprisingly able to provide. And much more.

Not all "firsts" appealed to her though. When, on their first night together, after several rounds of avid, mostly silent lovemaking, only interrupted by occasional obscene words, he said to her, "You are my first redhead," she felt like slapping him hard in the face. His tone made her feel like some kind of a milestone in a sexual oddity bucket list. Redhead: check. Next target: woman with no belly button.

However, she contained her ego and just replied in a calm voice:

"And you are my eleventh infidelity."

He burst out in a loud laugh, too loud to be genuine. She smiled inside because she knew she had succeeded in provoking him back. However progressive a man is, he'd still hate not being the frontrunner of a race. Boys have to compete. Precede. Win. Especially when the trophy is a woman's body. Man has been bred to see the latter as a trophy for centuries, often by the woman herself. It is an instinct that feminism might never be able to kill once and for all. Whatever the laws, no matter the level of evolution in a given society, there will always be a caveman inside many suited and well-mannered men, pounding his chest and howling, "I did it! I did it!" before dragging the female away by her hair.

The trick, in the twenty-first century, is how deep the man can bury him. Or how well the woman can tame him.

Men consider that being a married woman's first adultery is as significant as being a virgin's first ever sexual relationship. Even more significant. The moral impediments and the guilt are harder to overcome in the first case. It is, after all, an "official" sin—*Thou shall not commit adultery*—and it involved destroying another person, whereas virginity is more of a social patriarchal construct. Thus, the first challenge is greater. But once that step is taken, it becomes a lot easier for the man. And addictive for the woman. A slippery slope. Just like chocolate.

Qadar knew that all too well. She had lied: Omar was way past her eleventh Lindt bar.

"So you're one of those women who count their men? Tell me, do you have a secret diary with their respective names written on it, and little flowers and hearts drawn all around?"

"No. But I do have a secret diary with their respective penis sizes."

It was like a sword fight between them, and she was immensely relishing it. She'd always wanted to practice fencing, but she learned to do it with words instead of sabers. The blades of language were sharper anyway. Omar scowled for a split of a second. *Touché!* she thought.

When she finally introduced herself after the fifth orgasm, Omar was intrigued by her first name, quite unusual for a Lebanese.

"Where does it come from? Do you have a Saudi parent?"

"No. I've earned it!"

He burst out in laughter.

"You must surely know that redheaded women were suspected to be witches. I wonder if that's why I chose you: you must have bewitched me."

"Firstly, I am the one who chose you. Secondly, I don't mind being burned at the stake, so what are you waiting for?"

She had once read that all redheads were descendants of Vikings. She did some research and found out that Viking warriors had indeed been to Turkey, somewhere around the tenth century. They allegedly reached Constantinople (Istanbul) with two thousand ships, but they never succeeded in conquering the city. They did, however, infiltrate it and its surroundings as merchants, and have even left cryptic marks in *Hagia Sophia*,[20] which can still be seen today. Did a Viking leave a mark in one of her female ancestors' vagina? Is that where the curly red hair that she shared with her maternal grandmother came from? This rare mutation had skipped a generation between them. Her mother's was blue-black, and as straight as a silk curtain.

On their fourth night together, he asked her to take off her wedding ring whenever she was with him. "I somehow intuited there was an old-fashioned man hidden under that crust of cynicism," she remarked teasingly. Her mocking didn't make him feel uncomfortable. He was too self-confident to ever get embarrassed. He just held her hand, took the ring off himself, and calmly put it on the bedside table.

Could he be falling for her? And most importantly, could she be falling for him? She let herself slip toward that cliffy thought for a second. But she quickly swept the absurd idea away, and allowed his kisses to take her elsewhere. *No, Qadar!* she reprimanded herself.

She thought she was immune to *gharam*, strong, passionate love. But the truth is, she had unconsciously wished for it too ardently, too frequently, and too vainly, to dare and expect it at the age of thirty-five.

She just didn't know that yet.

⟵

Beirut —Sunday, June 12, 2005

In the beginning came the realization.

The painful realization that my parents' marriage was everything but a happy one. It was a ruthless, relentless psychological warfare

....

20   A Greek Orthodox Christian patriarchal basilica, turned into an imperial mosque, and now a museum, in Istanbul, Turkey.

$\diamond$ $\heartsuit$ $\spadesuit$ $\clubsuit$

that devastated the household brick by brick. What gave it away first and foremost was something beyond tangible proofs, like an instinct, a scorching feeling in my gut that kept telling me things were not OK.

In the beginning came the realization (they don't like each other). Then the denial (they will work it out). Then the capitulation (that's how it will always be). Then the accusation (it's all his/her fault). Ultimately, most destructive of all stages, came the self-shielding process. Unconscious. Subterraneous. Cruel: real, lasting love is a chimera. Marriage sucks. People are not made to be with each other forever. Plan B is a must.

And C. And D…etc.

Until three months ago, I've always been able to walk away. I say "able to" while the right expression should be "unable to not." The terror of being abandoned was stronger than any potential bond and the perks it brought with it. The heart that I was stretching out was continuously hesitant, shaky, retractable at any sign of danger. And I made sure that this spinelessness of mine was well hidden, even to me. I used "I love you" in ways that deprived it from any meaning. I convinced myself that "this" was freedom, this inability to connect, to commit, to crave, to miss, to exalt. Enslavement had specific synonyms: attachment; involvement; connection; closeness; loyalty; jealousy; union; fusion; possessiveness; openness; expectations. In short, any feeling that is even remotely related to a real love relationship. And it had to be avoided at all costs…If I cheated, it was just a proof that I was free. If I left, disconnected, turned my back, it only meant that I was a liberated, untamable spirit.

But now I know I was merely terrified.

Funny how many veils there are to help conceal the truth. Finally, when real love arrived, the devastating, overwhelming, unavoidable kind, I let the tsunami sweep me off, wash me up, suck me under, turn me over. It felt like being inside a washing machine with the drum on full power: soak, heat, agitate, drain, spin, twist, contort, wring…

I should go back to Aleppo tomorrow. I've already been away for too long. Away from the kids and from the boutique. But Samir Kassir's[21] assassination ten days ago, and the new wave of demonstrations that followed, have kept me from leaving. The brave, sharp, unapologetic Samir... Another Lebanese dream has died. No, it didn't die. It's been murdered. One of the Assad regime's countless crimes, past, present and future, in Lebanon.

It all seemed so surreal and absurd, me protesting against the Syrians in Beirut, while I was married to a Syrian man who was waiting for me in Aleppo. But isn't that how life is? Impeccably surreal and absurd?

Maybe I was not just protesting the presence of the Syrian Forces in Lebanon. Maybe I was also protesting the presence of my Syrian husband in my life.

And amid all of that, I witnessed my very own Big Bang.

Omar happened.

~

Qadar Barsom was born on a warm September day in the year 1970. Her father Luqa wanted to call her *Shapirta*, meaning beautiful in his native Assyrian. But her mother Qana strongly refused. "What kind of a weird name is that? Kids will make fun of her."

Luqa tried hard to sell it to her: "But Shapirta sounds so much like Rita!" He knew she loved a famous poem by Mahmoud Darwish, entitled "Rita and the Rifle," which he had made her discover a couple of years earlier, in one of his innumerous love letters to her. But she wouldn't capitulate. Qana was a tough woman, not one any husband would want to argue with, especially not during a hormone-flooded pregnancy. So he suggested *Yalda*, another Assyrian name.

....

21   A Lebanese anti-Syrian journalist (1960–2005).

◇ ♥ ♤ ♧

"Are you trying to upset me on purpose?" Qana objected.

Yalda was in fact too close to *Yaldiz*, a famous Turkish name. Lebanese people used the expression "*Metel Asser Yaldiz*" (like the Yaldiz Palace[22]) to refer to a lavish house.

"No child of mine will ever have a Turkish sounding name." Then she firmly declared, "We will call her *Qadar*—destiny," and that was the end of the discussion.

Luqa claimed the right to call their second baby whatever name he wanted, and Qana was quick to agree. Little did he know that she had already decided, for both of them, that they would have one child only.

Luqa Barsom, Qadar's father, was born in Ashrafieh district in 1943. But his parents were from Mardin, a city in Southeastern Turkey and had fled to Beirut in the second decade of the twentieth century because of Ottoman persecution. He took pride in having been born on November 22 of that year, the day Lebanon had achieved its independence. "Stop bragging about it! It's not like you chose the date yourself!" his mother teased him.

His parents, who weren't natives of Lebanon like he was, obtained the *tazkara*, the Lebanese identity card, many years after he did. At first, Assyrian and other Christian refugees didn't possess the Lebanese nationality. In 1958 however, then president of the republic Camille Chamoun initiated a decree to offer every member of a minority group Lebanese nationality, if fulfilling the condition of a ten years stay in the country. Luqa's parents did, so they applied for the citizenship and obtained it shortly afterward.

Qadar's mother, Qana Barakat, was born in Deir Yassin, Palestine, in 1946. When violence burst with full force between

....

22   A vast complex of former imperial Ottoman pavilions and villas in Istanbul, Turkey, used as a residence by the Sultan and his court in the late nineteenth century.

Jews and Palestinians in 1948, her parents left Palestine for Lebanon. First to Marwahin, on the borders, then to Beirut. In 1961, Luqa's parents moved into an apartment three stories above the one where Qana, her sister Najat, and her parents lived in Bourj Hammoud. The Assyrian family already had a laundry shop under the building, and the daily commute from Ashrafieh was tiring Luqa's father, who had been having health problems for the past three years. Qana had just turned fifteen, and an ardent love story ignited between her and eighteen-year-old Luqa.

On April 13, 1975, Qana, Luqa and their daughter Qadar witnessed the start of a war. One of the vilest kinds. Not between Turks and Armenians, not between Jews and Palestinians, not between any two obvious enemies which antagonism can be understood even if objectionable.

This time, it was to happen between brothers. Christian Cain and Muslim Abel. Muslim Cain and Christian Abel.

Both Lebanese. Both ready for a blood orgy. Both being cheered into it by external powers.

↩

Beirut—Monday, January 19, 1976

Yesterday has been a long day and night at the shelter, under the building where my aunt and uncle, Amto Muna and Ammo Naum, live. Well, it's not really a shelter. It is rather a spacious and humid warehouse situated on the underground floor, where mice and cockroaches played hide and seek with us. Their proliferation was helped by the fact that there is a bakery located on the ground floor of the building, one with very low hygiene standards.

I used to speed up my steps every time I went to visit my aunt and had to pass in front of the bakery's back door. The back door was always open, and there was a hideous old man working there, who never missed the opportunity to open the zipper of his pants whenever I crossed his way without my mother. I'd quickly close my eyes so that I don't see anything, but it was always too late. He kneaded the doughs with the same bare hands he used to touch himself. On special occasions, my parents would buy me a gateau from that bakery. And I'd eat it. Having an éclair was a rare luxury whose appeal was stronger than any feeling of repugnance.

One day I finally told Mama what he was doing, and she got extremely furious.

"Did the bastard ever touch you?"

"No, Mama, he just showed me his thing."

She immediately went to the bakery, stormed into the kitchen, and slapped and punched and kicked the hell out of him. She wanted to call the police, but the bakery's owner, who was his nephew, begged her not to. He promised he would get him treated and keep watch over him. We never saw him again.

While pounding the old man, Mother kept yelling "Take this, Ameen!" I couldn't understand why. His name was Kevork, not Ameen. But then again, Ameen is also what we say at the end of prayer. Maybe she was praying while beating him?

A few days earlier, informants had warned us that an escalation was expected in the fighting between the Phalanges and the Palestinians, in the Karantina area, which was very close to where we lived, so we had the time to get prepared. The depot, however sordid, was safer than our own fifth-floor apartment, located in a building facing my aunt's, with no underground space, and more comfortable than the stairs where we used to sleep when the clashes got too close.

My mother packed a few things, along with her small, black leather bag, the one she kept hidden in my closet. "Never tell your father about it. This is for you, should anything ever happen to me," she said. I also packed my own treasures: Martine at the Zoo, *the latest book Father had brought me, and two issues of*

Burda[23] *magazine which I took from Mom's collection.*

"What do you need this for?" Mother asked me, perplexed.

"I love looking at the pictures!"

"Fine, but make sure you don't rip any of the pages. I like to keep them neat."

Mother likes to keep everything neat. Sometimes I feel she'd prefer if I were a statue—"Don't step here!" "Don't touch that!" She mops the house's floor every two hours. She sees things nobody can see. Footsteps on the tiles. Finger marks on the walls. Dust under the dust. Grandmother is like that too, but she lets me touch and do anything I want. "Leave her alone, it's OK," she says to Mother whenever I wash my hands and don't dry them soon enough. Mother quickly comes and wipes the drops of water that trickle from my fingers to the ground. Then she dries my hands, squeezing them so hard that I feel she wants to break them.

As I woke up this morning and came out of the shelter, I tripped over something while crossing the road behind Mother, and almost fell. At first I did not know what it was. Then as I reached down to pick up the book and the magazines, I looked more closely. I realized that it was a man's arm. A whole arm, without the rest of the body. There was dried blood on the spot where it should have been attached to the shoulder, and pieces of flesh were dangling out. One finger was missing from the hand, the pinky one, the Singuf Singuf'[24] finger. I knew it was a man's arm because of all the hair on it.

I immediately noticed the watch. It was strangely intact and looked brand new. It was a silvery Casio, with numbers instead of minute and hour hands, just like my father's. Father had gotten his last year from one of his rich customers, and he was very proud of it. He taught me to count to twelve and to recognize the numbers, so I ....

23   A renowned fashion magazine, published since 1950.

24   Familiar gesture among kids in Lebanon when they have a row. They twist their pinkies around each other, expressing that they won't speak to each other anymore.

could tell the time on it. I really liked it.

So I knelt down and took it. I took it nicely, saying thank you before speeding up my steps to catch up with Mother.

"Where did you get this?" she asked me later.

"I found it."

I didn't want her to beat me up so I lied. It wasn't a lie anyway. I did find it.

Is the man's arm sad?

Will someone pick it up and hang it back on his shoulder?

⟶

Qadar got used to her parents fighting. The war she was witnessing inside the house was no less vicious than the war outside. Who knew that a torrid love story like theirs (eight years of courtship and mutual longing, her father had told her) would become such a living hell? She got used to it, but it gradually made her all rotten inside, like a fruit infested by worms. She couldn't stand the constant yelling (her mother's), the constant cross face (her father's), the mutual blaming, the days—sometimes weeks—of hostile silence in the house, when she'd become a mere messenger between them.

Money.

It was almost always because of money. "Cold and poverty are the cause of all problems," she heard her grandmother say.

At first Qadar thought all marriages were like that. But when she visited Nina's house for the first time and saw how deeply in love her parents still were after thirteen years of common life, it was a shock. A shock she was quick to absorb, overcome, and rationalize.

"They must be the exception that proves the rule," she told Nina. "Marriage kills love. It's either the deadly routine, or the dirty socks on the floor, or the house bills, or the kids' school tuitions, or the small grudges that gradually build up and become insurmountable mountains."

This skeptical outlook on relationships had made Qadar very pragmatic, while Nina grew up to become an incorrigible romantic. But pragmatism and romanticism would destroy them both, similarly.

Relationships tolerated no preconceived notions. No optimism, no pessimism. You just close your eyes and leap.

"Marriage is like a watermelon," her mother would tell her bitterly. "You cannot know if it's going to be good until you've cut it open, and then it's too late." Her parents' marriage turned out to be an especially unripe watermelon.

She vividly remembers one of their earliest fights. She was six years old. It was a hot summer day, and they were having lunch at her grandmother's house. Her grandfather Bassem was absent, out playing backgammon in a nearby café, like he did every Sunday.

They were talking about a man, a militia fighter named Bachir Gemayel, who opposed the Syrians. Her mother loathed him as much as her father loved him. Assyrians were among the first to join the Christian militias, and Luqa had many cousins and friends in the Phalanges. He was about to enlist too, if it hadn't been for Qana's violent objection. Also, Luqa hated the Syrians with all his heart and soul. He was convinced that Syria's leader, Hafez El Assad, was using the pretext of "intervening to put an end to the war" only to occupy Lebanon. The Syrian officials repeatedly stated that Lebanon was part of Syria and that the Syrian Army didn't need anyone's permission to enter Lebanon. The Syrian educational system taught Syrian children that Lebanon was a Syrian district. It outraged Luqa.

What started as an argument between the two turned

into full-fledged combat. Insults and accusations flew across the lunch table like bullets.

"All of our problems are the Palestinians' fault anyway. The war started because of you."

"No! The war started because the Lebanese are selfish, condescending, racist pricks."

Please stop shouting, Mama! Qadar secretly implored. She closed her ears, and so did her Aunt Najat. Qayah, who had been preparing coffee when the quarrel started and wasn't paying close attention, tried her best to calm them down.

"Come on! *Hadjiss, please!*[25] Stop this!"

Then she turned to Qana: "Trust me, *aghjikes*, my daughter. The Palestinians are no saints."

"Besides, you should know better than to fight because of some warlord... What was his name again?"

"Bachir," Qana said in a resentful tone.

"*Sheikh Bachir*," Luqa retorted, emphasizing the leader's honorific title.

The tray that Qayah was holding fell to the ground, and the four coffee cups shattered. Najat jumped, startled. Qana and Luqa stopped screaming instantly.

She quickly reassured them.

"It's nothing, don't worry. I just felt dizzy for a second. It must be the heat. *Kheir, kheir.*"[26]

Then she murmured, as if to herself, "*Sheikh Bachir, Bachir Kizlar Agha.* All Bachirs are criminals."

Only Qadar, who was helping her grandmother pick up the pieces, heard that last sentence.

....

25 Armenian dialect.

26 Arabic for "good." The expression is used in Lebanon when something bad happens, as a way to wish that something good comes out of it.

⌒

Beirut—Tuesday, April, 11, 1978

I didn't see anything at first. The sun that invades the small kitchen every afternoon was blindingly intense. I only heard my mother scream as soon as she opened the door.

Then I saw her. She was lying on the floor, wearing her favorite printed dress. Aunt Najat was kneeling next to her.

"Why are you lying on the floor, Tatiky?"

My grandmother loved it when I called her Tatiky instead of Teta.[27]

She didn't reply. Aunt Najat was trying to shake her but she wouldn't move. She didn't say "Batchik dour inzi,[28] give me a kiss," like she always did whenever I arrived. Was she sick?

There was a yellow container next to her. I spelled out the words written on it in black. I was very good at spelling. "R-A-T P-O-I-S-O- N."

I knew what "rat" meant. I hated rats. Except for Jerry, the star of my favorite cartoons. Jerry was funny and cunning, sneakier than Tom the cat. I watched them every evening at six-thirty on our television.

Actually, Jerry was a mouse, not a rat. Father explained the difference to me.

"What does 'poison' mean, Mama?"

Mother didn't answer. I turned and looked up. She was covering her face with her hands.

Then she shouted at me.

"Get out! Get out right now!"

What did I do? Was Tatiky sick because of me?

....

27   Lebanese dialect.

28   Armenian dialect.

◇ ♥ ♤ ♧

Tante[29] Elham, the next door neighbor, started knocking, alarmed.
"Is everything OK?"
Mother opened the door and shoved me outside.
"Keep her with you!"
Then everything became chaotic. From Tante Elham's flat, I could hear the mutters of other neighbors, the siren of the ambulance, the instructions of the paramedics.
Later it was all over and everybody left. That night, both Najat and I stayed at Tante Elham's house. Mama didn't even say goodbye to me.
Baba came to check up on me later. He said, "We will come back for you tomorrow afternoon. Be a good girl." And he hugged me tight.
Neither my father, nor Tante Elham would answer my questions. But I figured everything out on my own. I am used to seeing cadavers.
Goodbye, Tatiky.

⌐

Hell had a branch in Lebanon. It was called *Deir Al-Salib*, the Convent of the Cross, or as it was more commonly known, the "*Asfouriyeh*," madhouse.

It was a monastery, when it was first built around 1919, turned into a sanctuary in 1937, then into a psychiatric hospital/inferno in 1951.

It was early August of 1982. Bassem had died peacefully in his sleep at the age of eighty-eight, and Najat had become a problem. Qana couldn't just leave her alone in the house. Najat's psychological condition had gradually worsened since Qayah's suicide. She barely ate and would spend hours staring at the wall. Long years of Veronal, then Valium, intake had gradually destroyed her and turned her into a zombie.

....

29   A French word that the Lebanese, especially kids, use when addressing an adult woman as a sign of respect.

A friend of Luqa told Qana about the specialized hospital, which was located in the suburbs of Beirut. "They take good care of those people over there."

Najat was admitted into Deir Al-Salib on August 18, 1982. There she discovered a whole new dimension of the word "pain." Ice baths to calm her and the other inmates when they were being too loud and agitated. Electric jolts to stimulate them when they become excessively low and apathetic after the ice baths. An endless circle of abuse called mental treatment by that hospital's standards during those days.

Die then resuscitate. Resuscitate, then die. Again and again, until irreversible death becomes one's ultimate hope.

In the same way that prisons in Lebanon turned small or first-time offenders into skilled criminals, Deir Al-Salib turned the slightly depressed or mildly anxious into officially, clinically, conclusively "crazy" people.

When Qadar went with her mother to check up on Najat less than a month after her admission, the twenty-eight-year-old was looking, and most probably also feeling, seventy. Najat couldn't speak at first. She only cried, hugging Qadar tight and squeezing Qana's hand. She cried for a full thirty-four minutes. Qadar counted them on her Casio watch. Her friend Nina always made fun of that watch, saying it was too manly, but Qadar was very attached to it. The Casio on her wrist and the steel locket around her neck were the two things she never took off.

As the nun who had brought Najat to the visiting hall left briefly to answer a phone call, Najat whispered to them, "Please take me away from here. *Dakhil ijraykon*, I beg you!" She now had black hairs on her chin from all the Cortisone she was being given. Even her voice had changed during that month. It had become deep and hoarse, as if it was rising from a grave. The grave that her soul had become.

Qadar would never forget that voice for as long as she lived.

Having to listen to her mother explain to her own sister why she had to stay there was excruciating. How could she be so insensitive? She practically told Najat that there was no place left for her "outside."

As they were saying goodbye to her, promising to return soon, Qadar decided she wouldn't come anymore. She couldn't. She was haunted by the screams she overheard and the convulsing bodies she glimpsed in that horrible place.

But one day, many, many years later, she would vividly regret her weakness and selfishness. The shame of not having visited Najat would become harder to endure than the sound of the cries and the sight of the seizures. Worse than all the empty eyes that she had seen there once.

Were those eyes empty, or "emptied?" Qadar often dreamed that the nuns and nurses used spoons to scoop life out of the patients' eyes.

When they came out of the hospital, she turned and looked at her mother's face: it was imperturbable. As if she felt nothing. No love. No compassion. No guilt. *Is her heart made of stone? Does she even have one?*

"When will she get out of here?"

"I don't know."

"Can't she come live with us?"

"No."

"Why not?"

"Because she just can't. Stop asking so many questions."

Her mother's abrupt way of ending any conversation with her. Qadar was used to it. "Why did *Tatiky* kill herself?" "Why do you sleep in my bed and not with Baba?" "Why can't I have a brother?"

"Stop asking so many questions."

Ever since she turned four, Qadar started begging her

parents for a sibling. Not just any sibling. She wanted a brother, although she would have settled for a sister, too. Her father would smile and say "*Inshallah*, God willing." Her mother would ignore her plea. Every single time. Until one day, Qadar stopped asking.

The cab driver who brought them back home from Deir al-Salib told them that there had been an explosion in the headquarters of the Phalanges Party in Ashrafieh, and that there were rumors that Sheikh Bachir Gemayel might have been killed.

Later that evening, the rumor was confirmed, as Sheikh Bachir's body had been found under the rubble.

⁓

Beirut—Tuesday, September 14, 1982

"Those *people*."

Who are they?

They are called the lunatics, the wacky, the nutty, the demented, the deranged, the insane, the maniacal, the bipolar, the psychos, the creeps...

The unfit for Her Majesty the Society.

The ones we should ignore, forget, avoid, repudiate, pity, shun, exclude, push away. Even though, most often than not, we are one of them.

Rather, because we are one of them.

"Those *people*," *we say, to keep them in a separate dimension. There's "us," and then there's "those people." We convince ourselves we are safe.*

"Those *people*," *we say, just like we also say "that illness" for cancer. "Ma'a min haydek el marad."*[30] *We do not name it for fear it*

....

30   Lebanese colloquial for "She has cancer."

might hear us, notice our existence and come for us.

But the truth is, we are all mentally ill. All stained. All imbalanced and sick and confused and messed up. All seven billion of us. To different degrees.

One can't be a living human being without having grown some form of mental disorder to counter the brutality of this world. To be able to justify it, or at least tolerate it.

It could be an obvious disorder, like schizophrenia. Or a well-concealed one, like religious faith: the ultimate collective psychosis.

The disorder is the Cure, not the Sickness.

The Cure for Life.

⸺

It was a Saturday and she loved Saturdays. It was her birthday, and she hated her birthdays. Her mother had baked a ring-shaped cake. That evening she'd stick thirteen little candles in it. Qadar would blow the candles, and it would be over. The famous yearly celebration of the day she was born. Qadar only looked forward to the new pack of books that her father would certainly bring her later that day as a gift. She had specifically asked him for one written by her favorite designer, Sonia Rykiel, called *"Et je la voudrais nue"* ("And I would want her naked"). She hoped that her conservative father would disregard the controversial title and surprise her with it tonight. She also hoped he'd be able to find it: it was published in 1979, more than four years ago.

She liked everything about Rykiel: her crazy red mane, obviously, but also and foremost her revolutionary designs, her liberating cuts, and her androgynous style. Qadar's mother, Qana, was always praising Coco Chanel. Sure, Chanel was remarkable; a ground breaker and a pioneer on so many levels, but she was too classical for Qadar's radical taste. So when she read an article about Sonia Rykiel in an issue of *Elle* borrowed from Nina's mother, she felt that she had found her role model. Furthermore, Rykiel's boutique in Paris, photographed in the same *Elle*, had a peculiarity that scintillated Qadar: The designer displayed books in her shop windows, not just clothes! She had somehow merged both worlds, and it worked. Qadar, who had always been torn between her two interests, literature and fashion, felt reassured at last: she didn't need to give up one for the sake of the other.

It was already early afternoon, and Qadar was immersed in one of her novels when Qana said, "I have to go somewhere and I need you to come with me."

"*Oor Gertangkor*, where are we going?"

She spoke to her mother in Armenian. Ever since her grandmother's passing five years ago, she became determined to learn her language. She already understood it quite well, growing up in a mainly Armenian community. It only took her six months or so to speak it fluently.

"To a doctor."

"Why? What's wrong?"

"Stop asking so many questions. *Hakvir*, get dressed."

Growing up, Qadar always felt closer to her father than to her mother. Despite the fact that she had things in common with both of them (she shared a love of fashion with Qana and a love of books with Luqa), her complicity with her mother was undermined. Firstly, she was forced to take sides in their quarrels, even if secretly. Picking a side can keep the children of failed marriages from feeling completely torn.

Kids perceive life as right and wrong, black and white. We aren't yet equipped to handle gray areas of relationships, to understand that sometimes "nobody is wrong," or "both are wrong." There has to be a tormentor and a victim. Later,

♢ ♥ ♤ ♧

of course, much later, we acquire the tools to digest what has happened and have to deal with the consequences of having favored one victim, or tormentor, over the other.

It was easier for Qadar to take her father Luqa's side because he was less of an obvious culprit in the fights. Her mother was a screamer, while her father was a quiet, sly provoker.

Screamers, she'd learn later, are the weakest in the aggression hierarchy.

Secondly, her father was rather laid back while her mother was pushy and domineering. "You will do this; you will be that." Qadar often felt like she was Qana's revenge from something, from someone. And while she was quite driven and determined herself, by nature, the weight of Qana's pressures and expectations would become sometimes too heavy to bear. Or rather, too exasperating. Qadar wanted to own her ambitions, not for them to be a reflection of her mother's aborted ones.

Also, Qana was violent and volatile, and she suffered from nervous breakdowns and control issues, especially after her mother's suicide and Najat's internment. Qadar knew that hittng kids was a common parenting style (many of her friends were belted when they'd mess up), but she was an obedient and respectful daughter. She mostly kept to herself and hardly caused any trouble. Still, Qana would beat her up for the silliest of reasons. Sometimes she'd even slap her awake in the middle of the night if she was tossing and turning in the bed that they shared. Qadar found it hard to forgive her. She had a rebellious spirit, and her mother was the only one to break her. Repeatedly.

As she was walking with Qana, Qadar's thoughts went to the novel she had been reading, or rather re-reading, that morning. It was *Little Women*, by Louisa May Alcott, one of her absolute favorites, and it was probably the hundredth time she'd read it. She especially adored the Jo character, who was rebellious and loved literature. Reading books, along with drawing her dress sketches, was Qadar's medication, and delving into *Little Women* always made her feel considerably better. "School is imperative but books are the real teachers," her father would always say to her.

Her father was mostly self-taught and way more mature intellectually than the brevet he held implied. He went to a public school on and off, but his real knowledge came from one of his father's cousins, who turned out to be an excellent tutor. Not only did he teach him to read, write and calculate in both Assyrian and Arabic, but he also gave him poems to learn by heart and philosophical notions to dwell upon. The cousin was an old and eccentric retired priest who never left his house without a hat and a cane. He spent the mornings painting and the afternoons strolling, his left hand folded behind his back, endlessly moving his fingers between the beads of his *masbaha* rosary.

Ever since Luqa turned seven, he would visit *Abouna* Father Gewargis twice a week in the early evening and take lessons about everything: history, geography, literature, philosophy, sciences... In less than five years Luqa accumulated more knowledge than a high school student by those days' standards. Three years later he got his Brevet degree and continued his education through books, while helping his sick father run the laundry place he had in Bourj Hammoud.

"*Hosseh*, here it is,"

Qana's unusually low voice frightened Qadar. They had reached their destination. They went up the first floor of a decayed two-story building. Stinking water was leaking from every corner of the stairway, and there were cockroaches everywhere. The main door of the clinic was open. They went inside a ragged room with beige plastic chairs and a disrupting neon light. Nobody was there, not even a secretary. The morbid hall led to another room which door was closed.

"Wait for me here. I should be done in an hour or so."

Qana knocked on the door. Someone opened. Qadar heard a man's voice but she couldn't see him from the angle where she had sat. Her mother went in and the door quickly closed behind her. Five or ten minutes of silence followed. Then the screaming began.

Ghastly. Formidable. Hair-raising.

Like a deer being being devoured by a lion would scream, if it could.

Like death would roar if death should ever announce itself.

Qadar stood up, ran toward the door and opened it in haste. She saw what no thirteen-year-old should ever see. Qana was naked from the waist down and had her legs parted. The man, who looked more like a butcher than a doctor, maybe because of the blood stains on his white coat, was bent between her thighs and stirring some kind of a huge needle inside her loins. Blood was trickling down into a dark green plastic bucket.

"Get out! Get out right now!"

Her mother kept shouting frantically even after she got out.

She knew very well what was happening. She had studied this in biology.

I could have had the sibling I always wished for. I'll never forgive her for this. Never!

There was too much to forgive already.

On their way back home, barely able to walk and leaning on her daughter, Qana turned to Qadar and said in a dry tone, "Don't tell your father about this."

—

Beirut—Saturday, September 24, 1983.

"I don't want a cake for my birthday, Mother. I just want you to stop beating me."

Will I ever say that to her out loud? She knows how to play the guilt card with me perfectly.

"I tolerated the intolerable because of you."

Every time she says that I want to scream in her face: "I wish you didn't! You ruined my life because you did!"

That's when I feel I have every right to hate her.

But then she would spend many sleepless nights bent over her Mercedes sewing machine, making an exact copy of the dress she couldn't buy for me, or the one that I had drawn myself. And I would feel like shit wearing that dress. It always felt like wearing a coffin. A coffin where my self-esteem laid, murdered by my guilty, or blackmailed, conscience.

The word "sacrifice" can be a weapon of psychological terrorism. One of the most harmful—and self-harming—addictions.

I can't remember why I deserved yesterday's beating. My eyes are swollen from all the crying. People on the street stare at me.

Ah yes! I had spilled cherry juice on my school uniform.

I once read about a species of small monkeys called the mustached tamarins, found in Brazil. The mothers in this species are known for their infanticidal tendencies. They pitilessly smack their babies, or toss them to the ground from high trees.

"Stop beating me. Stop beating me."

And today, this. This infamous crime.

Was I the tool of her vengeance against my father? She keeps saying he disappointed her. Isn't letting someone down a form of treason?

That is why having high expectations in a marriage is bad.

Marriage is the guillotine of dreams. Better be disenchanted in advance.

I've read Euripides' Medea, the play about the Greek princess who kills her children only to get back at her husband. My French teacher was incredulous when I told her I had read it. "This is way out of your league. Did you understand it?"

Of course I did! I am Medea's daughter, Mademoiselle Alice!

He gently touched her chin and she automatically opened her mouth.

"Is it going to hurt?"

He smiled. She knew she sounded like a little girl but she was terrified of dentists.

Dentists, gynecologists, and cockroaches.

"Just lay back and relax. I promise you won't feel a thing."

Those were the first words he ever said to her. His Syrian accent hit her like a bombshell. It did not mesh with his delicate features. There was a flagrant dissonance. Even though she had learned with time not to generalize about the Syrians like her father did, she still found it difficult to forgive their dictatorial regime for what it did to her country. Them, and others of course.

"Well, we've had more than our share of responsibility too," she thought. "Most probably the biggest."

She strived hard to be fair. The Lebanese very uncivil war had officially ended two months ago, in October 1990. Her reluctance didn't last long anyway. He had a warm, hypnotizing voice, which made up for the disagreeable accent that brought back the disagreeable war memories.

Fouad Yaziji was a quiet, serene, patient man, her complete opposite. He was the least talkative person she'd met, and he was also predictable and dependable. If there was an antidote to her overpowering recklessness, he was it.

She felt secure with him. Too secure. They started dating soon afterward. Clandestinely at first, because she dreaded introducing him to her father. Fouad spoke marriage to her after just six weeks of their first encounter, or rather, of her first appointment at the clinic where he worked. It was quite an expensive clinic, actually, and she was grateful that her parents had managed to send her here despite their difficult financial situation.

"How about we get married?"

He just blurted out the question while he was fixing her wisdom tooth. *So much for a proposal,* she thought, a bit frustrated. But she already had no qualms about him ever acting romantic, and she even valued him for being this practical. She was eager to leave her parents' house, so she immediately said yes. She didn't actually say the word. She couldn't, with her mouth wide open and her tongue completely numb from the heavy anesthesia. She rather squeezed her eyelids and that was it.

Qadar wasn't in love with Fouad, but she liked his company, or rather, the effect that his company had on her. It soothed her. "He is the Panadol to my fever," she said to Nina when she told her about the nonproposal. Her friend wasn't convinced by the unemotional description.

"You should marry someone you love!"

"Yes, I should indeed, because that worked so well for my parents, didn't it?" she replied sarcastically. "Thanks, but no thanks, Nina. Love is for those who lack imagination. Or have too much of it."

"You will end up hating him for the same reasons you like him now."

I already know what's in this watermelon, Qadar thought. *No high expectations mean no distress.*

◇ ♥ ♤ ♧

Fouad was also well-off, and that was a key advantage. Her father's laundry place had slowly gone back to business, but Luqa spent most of his time reading or playing cards with his friends in the backroom. He had become addicted to *Tarneeb*, a plain trick-taking game like whist or spades. Another reason for him and Qana to fight, as if they needed one more! The house's atmosphere was more suffocating than ever.

As soon as Qadar understood what the word "divorce" meant, she secretly kept wishing her parents would get one. Do couples who fight know how much damage they cause to their kids? Do they know how selfish they are, staying together, using their sons and daughters as a pretext? Do they realize that "till death do us part" can become a death wish in their children's souls? Damn the hypocritical societies that prefer a fake status quo to a healthy and neat separation, and damn the cowardly mothers and fathers who submit to such social and religious standards.

Life is too short for conventions.

On April 28, 1991, only a little over four months after they had met, Qadar and Fouad were already married. Her parents opposed the idea at first, especially her father. Her mother's objections disappeared when she learned that Fouad was financially comfortable. That's all she's interested in," Qadar thought. *Massari, massari*, obsessed with money.

"You're too young to get married! And what do you know about this guy? You've practically just met!"

Her father was fuming. Still, she resisted and insisted until he yielded. She knew perfectly well the real reason why he didn't want "this guy" in particular to be her husband. The same reason why she had been reluctant to introduce them to each other.

Fouad was originally from Aleppo, but his parents had moved to the Syrian port city of Latakia before he was born.

After he finished high school, they chose to send him to the prestigious American University of Beirut, despite the unstable situation in Lebanon. Its school of dentistry was one of the best in the Middle East, and his wealthy family could easily afford it. They were also well connected to many political families in the country, and more than one influential strongman, *Za'im*, had vouched to watch over him.

Fouad graduated in June 1989 and decided to keep on living in Beirut, despite his parents' growing fear for his safety and persistent pleading for his return. Only a few months earlier, the Lebanese Armed Forces Commanding General, Michel Aoun, had launched a "war of liberation" against the Syrians and their Lebanese militia allies, and the capital was more explosive than ever. His father threatened to cut him off but he didn't capitulate. One of his professors had already recruited him for his prominent dental clinic in Ashrafieh. He left the AUB dorm and rented a small apartment near the clinic. He had become addicted to Beirut.

Beirut's unique magnetism was also its curse. It was the cocaine of so many Arabs. They couldn't get enough of it, but they also unconsciously resented it for subjugating them the way it did, and for being the only colorful spot in a mostly gray area. While they publicly lamented its destruction, many Arab leaders were secretly rubbing their hands together, feeling avenged.

We almost always begrudge what or whom we love too much. The enamored are willful jailbirds, and as such they are the most tragic and bitter of all prisoners. They haven't been forced into captivity. They enter that shiny jail deliberately, with a big smile on their faces, thinking it's an amusement park. And they often stay in it long after the merry-go-round has stopped turning.

The marriage took place in the Greek Orthodox Church of *Mar Nkoula*, Saint Nicholas, in Ashrafieh. It was a very low-key ceremony, which only the indispensable people attended: the bride and groom's parents; Nina, who was also Qadar's bridesmaid; Fouad's childhood friend Fadi who came from Latakia for the occasion, in addition to some close family members and a few other selected guests.

On her wedding day, Qadar was two months away from graduating in design from the Lebanese Academy of Fine Arts. There were no proper fashion design schools then in Lebanon, and Alba's design program seemed the closest, and the most useful, to her field of interest. The academy was way above Qadar's parents means, but her Aunt Muna was the cook at the dean's house, and his wife liked her. The dean agreed to offer Qadar a scholarship, once he saw her progressive sketches and her excellent school grades, provided she'd do some paperwork every day after classes until she graduated.

Fouad had previously suggested they move to Latakia right after her graduation, and she had agreed. He had patched things up with his father, and he wasn't happy any longer in Lebanon. Hatred of the Syrians was becoming more acute than ever, especially after Aoun's defeat by them and his forced exile on October 13th of the previous year. Fouad could feel the rancor in every day's simplest details, a cold frown here, a barely subtle gaze of contempt there. Also, his uncle, who was a dentist himself, had established a clinic in Latakia and had been urging Fouad to help him run it.

Qadar, on the other hand, didn't mind being as far away from her mother as she could. She had heard that Latakia was a charming coastal city. She insisted only on two conditions: that they'd live in a house by the beach, and that she'd look for a job there.

"You don't need to work."

"You know me better. To me it's passion, not just work."

"*Mashi*, fine."[31]

Fouad hated disputes, another reason why Qadar had so enthusiastically agreed to marry him. What he couldn't solve peacefully, he would simply dismiss by assenting. It was very convenient for her. She didn't suspect that one day the dust under those indulging carpets would become too thick to ignore.

They moved to Latakia on the first of July 1991, to a house by the beach, just like she wanted. Less than a month later, Qadar was already working as a design assistant to a renowned Syrian stylist. She had her mind set on starting her own line and opening her own boutique once she had accumulated enough experience.

A boutique where she'd sell clothes—*and* books, obviously.

↢

Latakia—Friday, September 6 1991

"Just lay back and relax. I promise you won't feel a thing."

The first sentence he ever said to me could very well be the sum up of our sex life. We've been married for more than four months now, and still, nothing. I feel nothing with him.

I feel nothing for him, actually.

Nina was so right. His unwavering poise gets on my nerves.

I look at him, and I see a flawless man. A man without apparent weaknesses, vulnerabilities and susceptibilities.

I look at our life, and I see a flawless life. A life without concerns, risks, and uncertainty.

But what is a man without apparent weaknesses?

Just an actor.

And what is a life without uncertainty?

....

31   Syrian dialect.

Just a scenario. A tedious predictable scenario.

I feel like I have been dragged into a movie, one I don't even like. And I should smile and say my lines and pretend everything is perfect.

If only he could be more considerate. More emotionally and physically available. He makes love to me as if he was following precise instructions in a manual. Then he turns his back on me and goes to sleep. Not once does he ask me if I've enjoyed it. As if it was evident that I would. Is it selfishness or denial?

"Le lit est tout le mariage"—the bed is the whole of marriage. Balzac was a genius.

My period is very late. Could I be pregnant?

Shouldn't there be some kind of a physical impediment to a woman becoming pregnant without having experienced an orgasm?

Gods, should they exist, must be sexist men.

⌐

Qadar opened the blue wooden shades, and all the noises and smells of the beach came in to her at once. Sharp, luscious, moist. It was a warm Sunday morning in March, and there was a couple strolling along the shore, their jeans rolled up, barefoot. Every now and then they'd stop, bend over, and draw something on the sand with their fingers—most probably a heart—but it was regularly washed away by the waves. The soil giveth and the water taketh away. Qadar kept following their silhouettes until they disappeared and she could no longer hear their giggles.

She had dreamed of this house for so long. A house by the seaside. As a child she used to tell her friends, "One day, I will have a white house with windows that look like endless skies even when they're closed."

Indeed, Qadar had dreamed of this house for a very long time. Well, not of this house specifically. But of a house, of almost any house, by the beach. Getting to live in one in Latakia, Syria, was not exactly the way she had imagined her fantasy would eventually turn out. She grew up a Christian in a war-torn Beirut, and a Christian girl growing up in a war-torn Beirut would not normally dream of a house by the beach in Syria, that is, the "Enemy." She didn't even dream of one in *Rawcheh,* on the western, mainly Muslim, coast of the capital (*Bayrut el-Gharbiyeh,* as her mother Qana still insisted on calling it). She was rather hoping to be able to live some-day in *Jounieh,* or *Jbeil,* or even *Amchit,* all mainly Christian Lebanese coastal cities.

It wasn't until she was twenty that Qadar went to *Bayrut el-Gharbiyeh* for the first time. Before that, it was just a photo-graph on a postcard, or a vague place that her father would talk about sometimes, when nostalgia hit him. He would also tell her about Cinema Capitol, one of the most popular cinemas in Beirut's golden era;[32] alluring *Souk al-Tawileh,*[33] and other mysterious places with abstract names that she couldn't relate to. Whenever her father strolled down memory lane, she used to feel like an alien. Her Beirut was not his. Hers was a city of terror, destruction, and violence; his, a city of freedom, thrill, enlightenment. There was a gap, clean-cut, between the two. No connection, no build up. She might as well be from another country, with a totally different capital. Every time she heard the expression "Paris of the Middle East," which is how Beirut was known, she felt like throwing up.

She envied her parents at times, because their reminis-cences of the pre-war days could alleviate the horror of the
....

32 One of the most popular cinemas in Beirut's golden era.

33 A prosperous commercial street in downtown Beirut before the civil war, dating back to the Phoenico-Persian period and that once led all the way to the harbor. Other similar renowned streets were Souk al-Franj, Souk al-Sagha, and Souk Ayyas.

postwar era in their minds. They could always look forward to the past, especially her father. It was a comfort she didn't inherit. But she liked that break between their concept of the city and hers. It went well with her exploratory penchant. *It's so fortunate that memories cannot be exported from one generation to another*, she thought cynically.

Little did she know that memories, especially the burning ones, become encoded in our genes.

Her friend Nina—with whom she went, for 14 straight years, to a Catholic school run by nuns—used to laugh at her whenever they discussed their future plans and wishes, sitting at one of the white plastic tables in the cafeteria. "A house by the beach? What kind of a dream is that? Your hair will get all frizzy from the awful humidity."

But Qadar didn't mind the awful humidity nor the frizzy hair. She just absolutely needed to be close to the sea. It was a promise she had made to herself as a child, on the balcony of the modest apartment she grew up in, in one of Beirut's poorest areas. A balcony that overlooked nothing but other deteriorated buildings nibbled by bullets and bitten by rockets.

She frowned every time she remembered her childhood, especially her school days with the nuns. Qadar harbored a severe loathing for the so-called "brides of Jesus." The years she had spent among them had made her discover their duplicity, greed and inhumaneness. There were a few kind and compassionate nuns of course, but those were a limited edition. "Brides of Jesus, *mon oei!*[34] The Lord badly needs some marriage counseling," she'd sarcastically repeat to a horrified Nina. Her friend was a devoted Maronite, and the slightest irreverence to religious symbols or figures scared her. "The flaming fires of hell," a disturbing special effect in Catholicism, daunted her.

....

34   French equivalent of the expression "My ass!"

"Oh come on Nina! God must surely have at least some sense of humor. Have you seen Sister Constance's nose?"

Qadar took one final look at the Mediterranean Sea, inhaled its chaotic beauty, then closed the shades ruminating, *"This house is probably the only thing I sincerely like about my marriage."* "Shut up, Qadar! He's a good man and you're an ungrateful brat!"

She was used to having long conversations with herself. As she lied down again, waiting for Fouad to come with the usual cup of coffee he brought to her in bed every morning, she felt the baby's strong kicks.

"So you've woken up, my little genie?" she whispered, smiling. She caressed her tummy and said, "I know you're impatient to get out of this magic lamp. One more month my love. One more month."

Was she going to be a good mother? One thing she knew for sure: She would never lay a hand on a child of hers...

At that exact moment, Fouad came in. He had no cup of coffee in his hands and his face was unusually red.

"We are moving to Aleppo next week," he said. *Debbi kalakishik,* pack your stuff!"

He immediately left the room without even glancing at her.

"He knows," she thought.

It was a warm Sunday morning in March 1992 when Qadar started paying the price. The price of being a pragmatic in relationships.

⟶

Latakia—Thursday, March 19, 1992

"Is he mine at least?"

His first words to me in four days. I had just finished packing and folding all the new clothes I had sewed for the baby. I was sitting on my side of the bed, rubbing my belly with olive oil. The question must have been consuming him ever since he found out.

"Yes."

"How can you be sure?"

"Because it started after we knew I was pregnant."

"Tfou aleki, you disgust me."

He said it calmly, without raising his voice, yet it stung way more than a scream, than a slap. I disgust myself too, but I've been so, so lonely here. Lonelier with him than I've ever been.

There are people whose company sharpens solitude's knife.

Stop justifying yourself, Qadar! He is a good man and you're an ungrateful brat!

I know he's a good man. I know. But is a good man enough? Should he be?

If yes, how come so many good women in the world are never enough? Why are men's infidelities more socially acceptable? Theirs are "indiscretions," while women's are "betrayals."

Apparently, there's a gene responsible for that. And more men have it than women. I bet that the person who came up with that study's findings was a man. An "indiscrete" man.

What defines infidelity? And what matters more, fidelity to oneself or to the other?

So many questions with contradictory answers...

He was his friend. And his Best Man. Such a cliché! How could you?

Ask him to forgive you, Qadar.

Is there something to forgive? And if yes, would I want him to forgive me?

Do I regret doing it? No. Do I feel debased? Yes. But by one thing only: The lies. The lies that often come with following one's impulses instead of one's mind.

His calm voice, again.

"Are you in love with him?"

"No."

"Lesh lakan *why then, Qadar?*"

Yes, why? I didn't even like Fadi. He was so self-centered outside the bed. But then again, Fouad was so self-centered inside it. They filled each other's gaps perfectly, but none of them filled the real void in me.

Beds. Two-by-two meters of heaven and hell, where so many promises are made and broken. A tumultuous ocean of ups and downs, yeses and nos. Fouad was our bed's iceberg, and I was its Titanic. Which one of us sank the other?

Why, Qadar?

Don't say sex. Sex is just a cover-up. A cover-up for that desperate search for oneness, that longing to forget our intrinsic loneliness.

If Fouad was a thoughtful lover, would I have still cheated on him?

Say it, Qadar, say it. I dare you.

Yes.

No.

Yes.

It was the thrill more than the act itself. That inebriating energy that makes life less intolerable.

It's my mother's fault. She loved making my father miserable. And I turned out just like her.

Stop blaming your mother for your defects. She has hers and you have yours. You are not a kid anymore.

Grow up, Qadar.

Do I have to?

The answer is in your loins.

Do all people cheat? There are statistics out there, but I don't trust them. Is monogamy possible? I mean willful monogamy, not the forced, artificial, "I can't do this to him/her" kind.

The feeling that a person is completely totally effortlessly enough. It must be magical. Intoxicating. Will I ever have that?

I read that fetuses are tremendously influenced by their mothers' experiences during gestation. Does this mean that I might give birth to a natural adulterer? Luckily it's a boy. Life is easier for infidel men in our part of the world.

Fuck our part of the world. Hypocritical, murderous, cowardly, unjust.

Fouad has decided to name him Boulos, like his own father. He started calling him Boulos right there at the gynecologist's clinic, as soon as the ultrasound had revealed the baby's sex. He was beaming with pride.

He knew I was wishing for a girl. To console me, he said that our first daughter shall be named after my mother. "She has such a beautiful name. One day we will visit Qana together. We will visit the Holy Land too, once we've kicked the Israelis out."

How little he knew me. How little I had let him know me.

"I'd rather call her Qayah, after my grandmother."

He grimaced. He didn't want his daughter to have a non-Arabic name. "How about Qamar?" he said. "Didn't you once tell me that it's the same? That this is how your grandmother was registered on her Lebanese identity card? Also, it rhymes with Qadar!"

Everything is the same, Fouad. And nothing is.

Will there ever be a Qamar after this?

⟵

"What was that name again, Grandma Elmas?"

Amal, Qadar's associate at the boutique she had recently started in Aleppo and her only friend in town, had invited her on that day to her paternal grandmother's one hundredth birthday celebration.

The old woman was quite a character. Qadar had met her before, during one of her visits to Amal's house. She was Turkish, from Adana, and had married a Syrian from Aleppo.

She had already survived her husband and four of her children. Born in 1896, she has witnessed so much of what had happened to the world in the twentieth century.

Qadar had an unwavering prejudice against the Turks, but it was hard not to like Nineh[35] Elmas. She was astonishingly lucid for a hundred-year-old woman. She had an outstanding memory and could recite the Quran by heart. Hundreds of poetry verses, too. And she was funny. After the customary cutting of the cake, which she had insisted on baking herself, she sat Qadar beside her and started telling her the story of her life.

"Come, let me bore you to death," she said to the young woman. "It is my birthday and I am allowed to choose a new victim."

The special occasion encouraged reminiscing, and Elmas surely had a lot to reminisce about. Qadar smiled. She didn't know why the old woman had chosen her out of all the people who had come to the party. Maybe it was just a coincidence.

Or maybe not.

Qadar was only half-listening though, distracted by her own thoughts regarding next summer's collection, which should have been ready last month. Distracted, also, by the thought of the new baby growing inside her. "It's a girl," the gynecologist had told her yesterday. Suddenly, a familiar sounding name in the old woman's story interrupted her daydreaming.

"What was that name you said?"

She had to repeat her question in a louder voice, as Elmas had hearing problems.

"*Beshir Kizlar Agha.* One of the most ruthless men I have ever known. And I have known quite a few of them."

....

35   Turkish for "grandmother."

◇ ♥ ♤ ♧

It was a name engraved in Qadar's childhood memory, even though she had never recalled it before this precise moment.

All at once, Qadar was six years old again, in her own grandmother's house, hearing her mutter while picking up the broken glass pieces, "All Beshirs are criminals."

"Who was he, Nineh?"

Elmas said it all.

The kidnappings, abuses, rapes. The common tale of so many Armenian women in 1915. Qadar had already done her research and read innumerous books about the genocide, but there were gaps in the story that nobody had managed to fill, especially since her mother Qana shared very little with her about it. To hear a live account from someone who had actually witnessed the horror from the other side of the power equation, and thus was logically more credible than the victims' side, was priceless. And incommensurably painful. Qadar could hardly hold back her tears.

As much as she found it difficult to exonerate the Syrians for what they did in Lebanon, and the Israelis for what they were still doing to her grandfather's homeland, Palestine, she however managed to have some degree of common sense toward the conflicts. It was the criminal Assad regime, *not* all the Syrian people. It was the radical Zionists (and their biased Western allies), *not* all the Jews. The Turkish, however, were another story. She absolutely hated them. With an utter, un-limited, unbending force. She brandished her discrimination against them unapologetically.

"All Beshirs are criminals..."

Was her grandmother one of this man's victims? Is that why she said what she said on that day? She couldn't have been. The dates didn't add up. She had Qayah's Lebanese identity card. She had stolen it from her mother's black leather bag. It states she was born in 1912, and she would have been a little girl in 1915.

But it was the same exact name: Beshir Kizlar Agha. Maybe her grandmother's birthdate was registered wrong, just like her name.

"My grandmother's name was Qayah and she was Armenian. Was there a Qayah among the abducted women you met at this colonel's palace?"

"No. No woman was called Qayah."

"Are you sure? Maybe there was and you didn't know her."

"Of course I'm sure! I knew all of them. And the name isn't a common one."

Qadar was already dismissing her suspicion. Elmas fell silent. But then:

"*Lahza*, wait a second…"

"Yes?!"

Qadar could hardly breathe.

"Now I remember…There was a sweet little girl called Qayah. She was the daughter of one of the Armenian captives."

This made more sense. Was Qadar about to discover something big about her grandmother? She was obsessed with her. She spoke to her whenever she was feeling disoriented and needed guidance. Her bad relationship with her own mother had transformed Qayah into the real mother figure in her life.

The day right before Qayah committed suicide, she had told Qadar, "I want you to have this. It is the only relic I have from my mother."

A steel locket, it had hung permanently around Qayah's neck. Qadar would play with it whenever she sat in her grandmother's lap. Qayah took it off and put it in Qadar's hands.

"What was your mother's name, Tatiky?

◇ ♥ ♤ ♧

"Her name was Marine. And my father's name was Nazar."

With those words, Qayah was two years old again, saying devotedly the words that Hosanna was training her to say.

"My name is Qayah Sarrafian and I was born in Aintab. My father is a cobbler and my mother is a seamstress."

She quickly corrected herself: "Was, was. My father was a cobbler and my mother was a seamstress."

"I want to be a seamstress, too, *Tatiky*! Just like you!"

"…And like your mother! She's a wonderful seamstress, you know! Wasn't she the one who sewed you this lovely dress?"

Qadar ignored this last comment.

"Do you have brothers, *Tatiky*?"

But she had a fixation with brothers.

Qayah hesitated.

"I did, Sirelis. I did. Two. Hagop and Nerses. I also had two sisters. Maria and Hosanna. In fact, this locket contains locks of their hair, as well as mine."

"Did they have red hair like you and me?"

"No, *hokis*, my soul. They all had blue-black hair, just like your Mama's and Najat's."

"Where are they now? Can I meet them?"

Qayah paused for a moment, then changed the subject, going back to the locket.

"As I was telling you, this locket is a gift from me to you. This way you will always remember your *Tatiky* if anything should happen to me. But you have to promise me something."

"What?"

"That you'll never open it."

"Why?"

"Because if you do, my brothers and sisters will fly away and we will never find them again."

"I promise, *Tatiky*."

Qana intervened.

"Stop talking like that, *Mayrik*. Nothing is going to happen to you. *Salemit albik*, may you be safe."

Qadar vividly remembers her mother's eyes that day. They were red. Qadar thought they looked like two red raisins. When she and her mother first arrived at her grandmother's, the two women sat for a long time in the kitchen whispering, while Qadar was in the living room, playing with the neighbor's cat who often sneaked in from the balcony. Then, after an hour, they came out of the kitchen, and Qana's eyes were swollen.

Two weeks after her grandmother's death, Qadar asked her mother about the locket.

"Where is it? *Tatiky* wanted me to have it."

"I took it from you that day, remember? I am keeping it in a safe place, so that you don't lose it."

"I won't lose it. I want it and I want it now!"

That might very well be the only time she really stood up to her mother…

Elmas' voice brought Qadar back to the present.

"Yes, I remember Qayah very well. Her mother tried to escape and got killed. Poor woman. I was told that the little girl has survived though."

Elmas teared up.

"I looked after Aslan for three years before I got married and left the palace. He cried so much when I left."

It was all too confusing. Who was Aslan? Maybe Elmas wasn't as lucid as she seemed to be, and she was mixing different stories.

"Who's Aslan, *Nineh* Elmas?"

"Qayah's half-brother. The son that Marine had from Beshir Kizlar Agha."

Then Elmas looked up at Qadar and her eyes sparkled, as

if she was seeing her for the first time:

"Both Qayah and Aslan had red hair, just like you!"

Qadar ran to the bathroom and closed the door. She had to open the locket. She had to. Her grandmother would forgive her.

Her hands were shaking as she unlocked it. There were several locks of hair inside, just like Qayah had told her, each tied with a string.

She counted them. There were six in all.

Six, not five.

Four were blue-black, and two were red.

Beirut—Tuesday, February 3, 2004

When did I start hating him?

Probably when he forgave me twelve years ago, the day Boulos was born.

I really tried to make it work. For five years I tried. But the effort was becoming too costly for my sanity and my self-respect. So I stopped. Right after I gave birth to Qayah. He calls our daughter Qamar, and I call her Qayah. I made sure she'd have both names on her birth certificate, and he accepted as long as Qamar came first. Qamar Qayah Yaziji. Now I have two kids with a man I have absolutely nothing else in common with.

Only Beirut saved me. The city that I always refused to belong to, has finally become my refuge. I know that Fouad suspects why I like coming here so much. I keep telling him that I have to check on my parents. That Nina's husband has hit her again and she needed my support. That there is a fashion show I have to attend or a potential client that I have to meet. But I know he knows. And the fact that I know he knows has liberated me from the feeling that I was lying to him.

Sometimes I think he wants me to lie to him. I'm sure he presumes I am having affairs. But I am not.

I am having experiments. Good experiments. Bad experiments. Experiments that can be confessed. Experiments that can't. Experiments with men. Experiments with women. Only one of the latter sort, actually. With just one woman. That's how I discovered I wasn't into it. I just wish she'd stop texting me...

Beirut. The freedom. The possibilities. The power of a woman who wants to try everything and is not ashamed of it.

Am I happier now?

No.

But I forget more frequently how unhappy I am.

He kneeled down in front of her, took a deep breath.

"*Btetjawwazini*? Will you marry me?"

They were both bare naked and he had wrapped his strong muscular arms around her knees. *The arms of a construction worker*, she always thought whenever she looked at them.

"How did you get those arms? You're an intellectual!" she asked him more than once.

"Never underestimate the physical benefits of pretentiousness."

Omar didn't like intellectuals. He thought they were one of the most self-absorbed, self-important species on Earth. Maybe he was too hard on them only because he liked being too hard on himself.

"Will you marry me?"

It was so unexpected that it took her a minute to realize what he was actually saying. The magnitude of it. She was dying to say yes, hell yes, despite her skepticism about the concept, about the whole institution. Yet she didn't dare take him seriously. What if he was joking? She had recently told

◇ ♥ ♤ ♧

him that she had never been proposed to. Maybe he was just trying to make fun of her. They had been together two years now. Well, not really "together," but rather involved, as they had two separate lives in two separate cities in two separate countries.

B.O., as she had come to refer to her life before Omar. She used to think that this was the perfect formula. The further the distance between two lovers, the better and more durable their relationship. "Let there be spaces in your togetherness and let the winds of the heavens dance between you," she'd cite Kahlil Gibran, to convince the skeptical.

A.O., everything changed. Spaces, what spaces? If she could sew herself to him, she wouldn't hesitate. Many of her mindsets had turned upside down. Qadar had finally attained the most essential kind of freedom: not lying to oneself. *I was just a coward.* With him, she discovered that *one person can be completely totally effortlessly enough.*

"Couldn't we have met earlier, Omar?" she would sometimes ask him with a sigh.

"Love has no perfect timing, Qadar," he always replied, kissing her on the shoulder. That, along with the ritual of him gently taking her cotton socks off every morning, was a routine she adored. And it astounded her that she liked it so much, she who absolutely abhors predictable words and programmed behaviors.

Well, that was B.O., evidently.

Every time she used the abbreviations in front of him, he'd protest.

"Stop saying B.O. and A.O., *ya khawta*, crazy woman!" B.O. stands for body odor and A.O. means for Adults Only!"

"Well, you are 'Adults Only' material, you know! You should have that sticker on your forehead, just like they do with porn movies!"

"Did you hear me?"

He was still on his knees, gazing at her, his head slightly tilted back.

She laughed nervously and caressed his head.

"I am already married, *ya akhwat*, crazy man!"

He ignored her reply.

"Will you marry me, Qadar Barsom?"

He referred to her only by her maiden name, the name she also used for her clothing line. Barsom, not Yaziji. When Fouad had first seen the tags, he was livid.

Then Omar added, "I mean it."

He had intuited what she was thinking. He always did. It was intoxicating but also scary. "Get out of my head, *tlaa min rassi!*" she'd sometimes yell at him, exasperated. But it was tremendously liberating for her to feel that she could hide nothing from him.

She was still hesitant to take him seriously.

"You always said you didn't believe in marriage!"

"I don't. But I do believe in marrying YOU."

"Okay then."

"Okay then? What kind of a reply is that? I am not asking you to cut your leg off!"

She loved his sense of humor, especially at the most inopportune moments, when they were discussing critical or thorny subjects. It took the lid off her tense nature.

"I mean yes! YES, you fool! Of course I'll marry you! Then, coquettishly, "I already know which designer I'm going to wear."

"Good. So when will you leave him?"

He strictly referred to her husband as "him." Never once said his name.

When will she leave "him"? The hard question, head on. Omar was a man of shortcuts. He wouldn't twist and turn around what could be reached in a simple straight line. He had asked her that question many times before. Without the "getting married" part, though.

"I already told you. Not until the kids grow up."

He stood up and put his boxers back on.

"Kids? Grow up!? They are already grown up! You're doing to them what you wished your own parents never did to you."

"No, this is different. Their father and I don't fight nor scream at each other."

"So what? They know that you are estranged. Children always know, however hard their parents try to hide that from them. You're just using them as a pretext, Qadar!"

She knew he was right. She felt mortified for delaying the decision, she who always bragged about being resolute and autonomous, she who always criticized those who stayed in a failed marriage.

Besides, she was financially independent. She knew many women who were forced to tolerate their husbands because of money, but Qadar earned enough from her successful clothing line to live comfortably on her own. Even her mother had advised her to leave Fouad. "Life is too short, *ya binti*," she'd said. The whole dynamics of her relationship with Qana had reversed after they had opened up to each other; after she finally saw so many things that she was refusing to see. "I tolerated the intolerable because of you." Children do housebreak their mothers.

"You know how wicked he can become! He wouldn't let me even see them anymore."

Omar said nothing. He just sat there with a sullen face.

"Listen to me, *habibi*, my love. Boulos is leaving to the States in three years. He wants to study law at Duke University, and I'm sure he will get accepted. He's brilliant, and his father can certainly afford it. But I know Fouad, he won't send his daughter to America. I overheard him once telling his mother that he wants Qayah to follow the IB diploma program as a boarding student at the International College in Beirut, because it will increase her chances in being accepted at AUB. 'Qamar will become a dentist, just like me,'" Qadar mimicked her husband rancorously. Her dream was for her daughter to take over her fashion business one day, but she was wise enough to leave the decision up to her in due time.

"So as soon as she moves to Beirut, I will ask him for a divorce and follow her here. Remember this date: 19 July 2012."

"What is that?"

"The day Qayah finishes tenth grade in Aleppo and becomes eligible for the IB program in Beirut! The first day of our new life together."

"Are you crazy? That's in five years!"

"So what?"

Again, no answer.

She got worried. Was he in a hurry because he wanted kids? He always said he didn't, and he even had a whole theory about the necessity for people to stop procreating. But maybe he had changed his mind about that as well.

"Do you want a child?"

"Of course not!"

She breathed again, relieved.

"Then what's the rush? I'm going nowhere. And I am spending most weekends here with you, am I not?"

"I am done being your weekend man, Qadar."

◇ ♥ ♤ ♧

⌐

Aleppo—Tuesday, December 25, 2007.

It is Christmas day. Mother just called. Najat is dead. Yesterday she threw herself off the third floor of the building where she was interned in Deir al-Salib. My first thought was, Now she can finally rest. *Terrible but true. Her whole life has been nothing but a constant ordeal, especially after her forced internment. Twenty-five long years of serving a prison sentence for a crime she did not choose to commit: the crime of being born different.*

Mother implored me to keep the suicide a secret. No one should know. "Especially not Father Marwan," she stressed, the grumpy Melkite priest whose parish she belonged to, and who was to perform the funeral ceremony. Even though she had become an Assyrian on paper after marrying my father, she kept on attending Mass at the nearby Greek Catholic church. Father Marwan was strict and might deny Najat a church burial because she had committed suicide. His predecessor, Abouna Elias, who had officiated Qayah's funeral, was way more tolerant and open minded. He had told Qana and Bassem then, "Who are we to judge a child of God?"

I was about to say, "To hell with Father Marwan and anyone who regards hopelessness as a mortal sin," but I held my temper. There was no need to upset Mother more at such a difficult time.

Why do many people condemn suicide, consider it a taboo or a proof of gutlessness? Doesn't it require a whole lot of courage to decide for oneself that "it's time to leave"? It is not in any way less than the courage it takes "to stay despite everything." Are those who kill themselves just in a temporary state of insanity, not really aware of what they are doing, drunk with desperation.

No, suicide is an act of mindfulness, par excellence. You can't kill yourself without your consciousness being at least an accomplice, if not the act's master architect.

To keep on living is to give in to a state of being that we had no say in choosing. Deciding to die is to take on the challenge. It is to refuse yet another radical imposition and claim the power of choice in a fundamentally choiceless existence.

Does it require more bravery to slam that door shut ourselves, or to wait for the door to get shut in our face, knowing it surely will?

Goodbye, Najat.

It was a hot day in late May of 2012, and time in Aleppo seemed heavy and thick, almost like mud. It was not flowing; rather, it was rolling on her like a huge rock, crashing her back again and again.

The Syrian Civil War had unfolded a little over a year ago. Peaceful anti-Assad demonstrations that had begun in January 2011 gradually turned violent when the government started killing unarmed protestors in the southwestern Syrian city of Daraa, and other cities. By Friday, April 22nd, the "Great Friday," the protests became an official war, after the security forces killed more than 109 weaponless demonstrators in more than twenty towns across Syria, and the opposition started to take up arms.

Another April, another war, Qadar thought. Wasn't it peculiar that all the wars her family has witnessed, starting with her grandmother Qayah, had begun in April?

But Qadar was used to "peculiar." Destiny, after all, is always peculiar. And accepting incongruity as a life routine was her superpower.

Lately she'd been trying to ignore the news. It wasn't so difficult. There isn't any real "news" in an ongoing war. She already knew what would happen: More people would die on that day, more houses would be destroyed, more children were about to become orphans and/or cadavers...

What was Omar doing now? Would she ever see him again? The past five years had been an endless circle of breaking up and getting back together. Of "I can't live with you, can't live without you." Mostly the latter. The war wasn't making things any easier. Ever since last year, she hadn't been able to visit Beirut as frequently as she used to. The journey was becoming more and more dangerous. Then she remembered what her beloved grandmother Qayah used to say to console her on a sad day: "Never a road without a turning, Princess, never a road without a turning."

"When was your turning, *Tatiky*? Did you ever have a break?"

Yes, she did. One that lasted ten months. Qadar remembered what her mother told her about Qayah and Avi. "We are surely progressing in love's domain from one generation to another," she thought sarcastically. "Grandmother enjoyed it for ten months, Mother for three years, and I for seven so far. If we keep this pace, maybe somewhere around the twenty-second century one of our descendants will actually succeed in experiencing it fully, without tragic interruptions."

"Thank goodness Boulos left the country two years ago or they would have forced him to enlist."

She has been urging Fouad again and again to take them out of Syria: "This war is getting out of control! We must leave too," but he won't listen. Only yesterday she said to him, "Why don't we go to Beirut? You can easily work there and Qamar could study at IC, just like you always wished."

She used Qamar instead of Qayah on purpose to humor him. It was unlike her, but she had to resort to all available means to persuade him. It didn't work.

"Why? So that you can see your lover more often?"

He loathed her. Even though they had reached a tacit agreement on living separate lives, and he had an official girlfriend now, he couldn't bring himself to forgive Qadar. She had cheated on him *first*. This is man's exclusive territory and she had dared to steal it from under his feet. He wouldn't agree to give her a divorce. The first time she asked him for it was five years ago, when Omar first broke up with her. She had panicked, and the fear of losing him overpowered the fear of losing her kids. She told Fouad everything. He said no then, and he kept on saying no ever since. It was his way of punishing her. He was also punishing himself at the same time, obviously. But he preferred to endure misery rather than to satisfy her by granting her the freedom she so badly wanted. That was how much he loathed her.

"*Talak*, divorce? Keep dreaming!"

"We'll see about that when your mistress starts asking you for a ring on her finger."

She loathed him, too. But not only. He also repulsed her. He had become particularly pro-Assad after the start of the civil war, like many other Syrian Christians. The latter, who were one of the country's religious minorities, had always been in a precarious position, feeling as if they were temporary guests in their own land, and they were convinced that the anti-Islamist regime was their main protector. Especially now, in a country and conflict where Islamic extremism was quickly rising. To them, survival mattered more than the fact that Bashar el-Assad was a tyrant and a war criminal, just like his father before him.

She understood where Fouad's stance came from, but she couldn't bring herself to respect him anymore.

Besides, she was Lebanese. It was a quasi-natural instinct for her to abhor the Assad dynasty.

◇ ♥ ♤ ♧

Qadar turned the TV on, just in time to see, again, the disturbing images from the recent Houla massacre.[36] Children's corpses were lying on the ground, displayed like potato bags. Many channels had kept showing the dreadful scene round-the-clock since yesterday.

When will human suffering stop being a media scoop?

But then again, should it, she wondered.

It was media's eternal moral dilemma—exposing horrid realities or observing human decency. "Media's a vampire," people say. "It sucks victims' blood until it's dry." Would they prefer living in ignorant bliss, hiding behind some idea of "respect for human dignity?"

It's not the slaughtered three-year-old who should have to apologize for bursting people's comfort bubbles. The viewer is always part of the story, always an accomplice in the crime. No matter how "un-innocent" the media can be, blood is still on our hands, it's still up to us. How do we get from human to humane?

Damn the power lust that turns man against man and turns both into animals. No, not animals. Animals are better than this. They do not kill without a forceful reason. They only kill to feed themselves or protect their offspring. Man kills to sustain his ego. Qadar planted her nails in the palms of her hands, one of several self-destructive habits she had picked up over the years. So many innocent people were paying with their lives. "War is my destiny, I need to accept it," she kept repeating out loud, like a mantra, just to feel the impact of those hideous words on her ears, her skin, her lungs, stomach, pelvis...

She had become used to the symphony of combat, an outrageous thing to even think, but, it was true nevertheless. After

36 An attack that took place on May 25, 2012, in the town of Taldou, in the Houla region of Syria, a string of towns northwest of the city of Homs, where 49 children died.

so many years of training and alienation, first in Lebanon and now in Syria, she'd grown used to it. "*Ma'aleich*, no worries! I'm war-broken," she would tell Nina, who called weekly to check up on her, but also to unwind about her own violent husband.

She looked at her watch. It was only 11 AM, yet it felt like ages since she had woken up to more news of slaughtering and misery. She didn't feel like doing anything. Books seemed irrelevant, and her sketches totally inappropriate.

"I have to get out of this hell."

Many times she thought about taking her daughter and leaving everything behind. Never mind divorce. She would move in with Omar. The papers meant nothing. A real marriage is the commitment between two people. "Living in sin," most people called it in her part of the world, but she couldn't care less about what people said or thought. Yet, there was one obstacle, a major one, to this scenario.

Just like the little Qadar with her own parents, Qayah had picked her father's side. Qayah was only ten when Fouad sat her and her brother down, and blurted out everything to them, as a response to Qadar's demand of divorce. Her husband was weak like that, only capable of lowly, below the belt forms of retaliation. Boulos, who barely got along with his father, just said, "It must be your fault." Her daughter kept silent. "She already hates me anyway," Qadar thought. She knew that Qayah blamed her for being absent too often and too laid back in her parenting style. But Qadar wasn't like that out of indifference toward her children. She wanted to give them a living example of how a woman should have the right to follow her ambitions. And having been smothered by her own mother, she opted to allow her kids more freedom, space, and privacy, thinking it was the ideal form of education.

But there is no such thing as an ideal form of education. Children *need* to blame their parents, and they will always find ways and reasons to do that, whatever they had been provided or denied.

One day, when Qayah was about seven years old, her passive-aggressive reproaches toward her mother became straightforward. Out of the blue, she screamed "I hate you" at her mother, for some mysterious reason that Qadar never managed to get out of her. And Qayah kept saying it regularly ever since. At the same time, she stopped answering when her mother called her Qayah—"My name is Qamar, not Qayah!"

Was she her daughter's Medea? Will she realize one day that Qadar had her reasons, for better or for worse?

Was it the famous Electra complex, or are mothers simply harder to forgive?

＿

Aleppo—Thursday, July 19, 2012

We woke up to even more tragedy today. Aleppo is on fire. Even schools and hospitals are being bombarded. Both the rebels and the pro-government forces are fighting viciously for full control of the city, and we are besieged between them.

Have you ever been to Aleppo, Omar?

I know you hate Syria, but you can't hate Aleppo. You can't possibly hate a city that has spent its whole existence, its very old existence—since 6000 B.C.—resisting and fighting, just like you.

Halab Al-Shahba', it is nicknamed: the white, the resplendent, the feisty, Aleppo. Chosen base of the Storm-God. Do you know how many civilizations and empires have bathed in its sun? Can you conceive how many layers there are in each rock, how many shoulders have successively leaned against its walls? Alexander the Great once shed a tear here. Don't ask who told me. I just know.

We woke up to even more tragedy today, the day my new life with you was supposed to begin.

The day I realized it never will.

⟶

The phone rang. *It must be Mother*, she thought. It couldn't possibly be Omar. She was the one who always called him. It couldn't be Nina either. She only called once a week, and she had already called her yesterday.

"He poured the coffee pot on my legs. Boiling coffee, Dina. Thankfully there were napkins nearby and I managed to wipe it off before I got badly burned."

"When are you going to leave that prick for good! I told you that you could work with me."

"He would kill me, Dina!"

"No he wouldn't. You're just letting fear own you. Hang up now and go tell him it's over."

He had started beating Nina two months after they had returned from their honeymoon in Cyprus. The honeymoon was a wedding gift from Qadar. It was a cold Wednesday morning in December, and Nina had forgotten to turn the water heater on. She wasn't expecting the slap. It made her lose her balance and fall to the ground. Confused, she didn't get up immediately. He kicked her hard in her belly.

"You made me shower with freezing water, *ya sharmouta*— you slut!"

Another kick in her belly. He was still draped in his towel, dripping water on the floor, but he had put his black Ranger boots on. He deliberately wanted to harm her the most he could. The pain was excruciating.

Why was he doing this? She adored him. She gave up everything to be with him. Even her family.

"It's either him or us, Nazla."

"You're just snobs. You only reject him because he doesn't have money."

◇ ♥ ♤ ♧

"No, Nazla. We reject him because he's a drug addict."

"Ex! Ex-drug addict!"

She eloped with him on her twenty-sixth birthday. Only Qadar knew. "He is the love of my life, Dina."

"Why didn't you turn the water heater on, *ya kalbeh*—bitch!" the love of Nina's life shouted.

Three more kicks. The pain had become intolerable. Then she saw the blood. A stain on her pajamas, right between her legs.

It was a cold Wednesday morning in December 1996 when Nina started paying the price. The price of being a romantic in relationships.

The beatings became more brutal with time, with more frequent heroin injections and less steady jobs. She never knew how he managed to get heroin. Often she had to be hospitalized. At first, when remorse still had a place in his intoxicated mind, he would apologize to her the next day, even cry and ask for her forgiveness. And she would grant it to him, of course. "I promise I will change." And she would believe him, of course. The love of her life. That's what he was.

When she finally realized he'd never change, he had become too dangerous to be left behind. "If you ever leave me, I swear I will cut you to pieces, *ya ahbeh*!"[37]

She once went to the Maronite Spiritual Court to see if she could get some help in divorcing him. One of her eyes was completely swollen and shut from the day before's beating, and she had bruises all over her body. The cleric who received her told her to "be patient and pray." He asked her to revise her conscience and stop doing whatever she was doing that offended her husband this much. Then, when she insisted on wanting an annulment, he said, "Fine. But you must help me help you."

....

37 Arabic for "cunt."

133

She didn't understand at first. Then he got up, came and sat on the coach right next to her, and put his sweaty hand on her knee. It felt worse than being beaten up, for someone as devout as her. She stood up, revolted, looked at him with her one open eye, and left.

Sometimes, often, Nina felt grateful that she didn't have kids. That the monster had made her unable to.

"When, Nina? When?" Qadar would ask her relentlessly.

"On the 19th of July 2012. I'll do it when you do it. Sisters in everything, *ma hek*, right?"

July 19, 2012. Ever since Qadar told her about Omar's marriage proposal, they started calling it their common "liberation date." They would joke and make plans for their joint "divorce party." The date was yesterday. But Nina didn't even mention it in her phone call. She didn't want to put her finger in Qadar's wound. She understood her friend. If she had something to say, she'd say it. If not, it was useless to ask her.

The phone was still ringing. Qadar picked it up.

She had guessed right. It was her mother.

"Nina is dead. The bastard killed her last night."

⌐

Aleppo—Friday, July 20, 2012

Her voice. Her frightened voice on the phone yesterday…

"He would kill me, Dina!"

"No he wouldn't."

"Hang up and go tell him it's over."

"Stand up for yourself! Once you do that he will stop threatening you."

How pathetic our bright ideas are when it comes to harsh reality. It's so easy to imagine we know what a person is going through and how they should behave. So easy to give advice.

Easy to the point of deadly.

Do broken dreams sigh when they fall to the ground, like broken trees?

Goodbye, Nina.

[3]
QANA

(Deir Yassin, 1946 –)

Daughter of Qayah
Mother of Qadar
Grandmother of Qamar

"She whose arms have fought a million battles"

T he **Queen of Spades** is a valiant warrior, and a glaring example of authority. Incisive and determined, she needs to achieve in order to exist. Overdriven at times and very hard on herself, she would benefit from a lesson or two in letting-go. Her destiny is ruled by the **Will**.

Had the Tree really fallen?
Never! Not with our red streams flowing forever,
not while the wine of our thorn limbs
feeds the thirsty roots.
—*FADWA TUQAN*
Palestinian poetess

"*Bettrajjek.* For God's sake!"

She wasn't one to beg. Pride was her only luxury. She'd only had to do it once before. And it was for her daughter's sake. But this was as critical. Her sister's fate was now at stake.

"Absolutely not."

"Please, Luqa! She has no one else left in the world but me!"

"I said no. One crazy woman is more than enough in this house. Besides, didn't Daniyel tell you about some specialized hospital?"

Qana felt homicidal. But she swallowed both the insult and her rage. She'd make him pay for them later. She always collected her debts.

"They treat them very badly there. I've heard atrocious stories about that place."

"Not my problem. All I know is that she can't stay in my house."

"*My* house," he says. She's the one who has cleaned it. The one who has washed, cooked and tidied; the one who's spent sleepless nights painting the walls; the one who carried heavy buckets of water five up stories whenever they ran out of it, which was every single day. Up and down countless times, until her arms became so sore that she could hear them cry.

Still, it was *his* house, not *their* house.

Was Luqa really that heartless, or was he trying to get his revenge on her? But then again, revenge for what? If anyone should feel bitter, shouldn't it be her? He never keep any of his promises. Ever. Not a single one of them.

Was she too demanding, the way he keeps accusing her? Or was he too passive, like she keeps reproaching him?

Marriage is the place where love comes to die. But could she really call it love, what she and Luqa had had? Isn't it true that they loved the idea of love more than actually being in love? Their whole relationship was built on idealized images of each other, images that reassured their personal wants and vulnerabilities rather than reflected reality.

Once marriage lifted the delusions, as it always does, they finally saw each other. "*Dab el talej w bayyan el khara*"[38]—the ugliness under the shiny appearance had surfaced. Matrimony is the most classic "now you see me, now you don't" magical trick ever invented.

She was a tortured soul, and he badly needed to be a hero. Or to convince himself he was one. The noble knight who saves the poor damsel. But Qana had too strong a character for such a role. And her ferocious temper only fully revealed itself after their matrimony. She was more lioness than kitten. A deeply wounded lioness, no doubt, but a lioness nevertheless.

....

38   Lebanese saying, literally "The snow melted and the shit emerged."

◇ ♡ ♠ ♧

Luqa, on the other hand, was an eloquent dreamer, and Qana was a natural-born struggler. She already had the determination. She only needed a hand to pull her up, and she assumed he was it. She wanted to be a go-getter's inspiration. The wind beneath a visionary's wings. She did not know, then, that there is a big difference between reveries and ambitions: the will to take action, the drive.

Luqa, as it turned out, had none. He was a fatalist. "If it were meant to be, it will happen. If not, then there's no use fighting for it." The despicable excuse of the lazy, she thought. And this desolating truth, again, only emerged after their matrimony.

The more she pushed him to do something, the less he was compelled to even try doing it: the self-destructive counter-reaction of some people when pressured. Instead of feeling motivated, he felt castrated. Virility is a fantasy of the vulnerable. Erections, physical and non-, feed on applause, narcissism, unconditional adoration. Qana was bad at cheerleading. She did it with blame instead of encouragement. She was too eager; he was too laid back.

Once she realized that even the tiniest morsel of expectation was lost on Luqa, Qana concentrated all of her stirring energy on her daughter Qadar.

"You will study in a good school. You will have good grades. You will go to university. You will be someone. You will make money."

Money, especially—lots of it. Those who have suffered from privation wouldn't settle for less than excess. They need the surplus to feel secure. "Enough" is just not good enough. "Enough" is shaky; it could suddenly vanish. The smallest knock out from life and you find yourself going backwards.

Backwards was not an option for Qana.

Push, push!

"*Yalla*, let's go!"

To her satisfaction, the tough love approach worked. Qadar grew up to be a taker rather than a receiver. But there was one collateral damage to all the herculean intensity she kept investing in her.

Her daughter didn't like her.

Qadar never said it explicitly, but Qana could sense it. It didn't simplify things that she was not the expressive, tender type of mothers. She showed her feelings with actions and practical forms of attention, not with hugs and cuddles and sweet words. She didn't mind that Qadar was hostile towards her. Or rather, she was willing to pay the price.

"One day she'll understand. And even if she didn't, it doesn't matter. As long as she doesn't have my kind of life."

Accomplishment is more vital than infatuation. What did infatuation bring Qana? Nothing but serial disappointment. It was her mistake, too. She had put all of her eggs in one basket, and now the basket had tumbled to the ground and all the eggs were smashed under her feet. Qana's frustration was crushing her. Her frustration *was* her. She cultivated the art of resentment. Naked, undiscriminating resentment toward everything and everyone. But she wouldn't give up on the future. On her daughter's future. Her own, she knew, was behind her.

⟵

What was she going to do with Najat now? She couldn't possibly leave her alone in their parents' empty apartment. Even though her father had become very old and weary in the past four years since his wife had died, he still managed to watch over her sister. To make sure she ate and took her meds. Now Bassem was dead too, and Najat was as forlorn as a desert tree. Qana inquired with the neighbors, to see if there was a room to rent in the building where she and Luqa lived, or if anyone was planning to move out soon. This way Najat would be nearby and she could check up on her easily. There was none.

Only one alternative was left: an inhumane one.

Deir al-Salib.

"Maybe it's not really that bad," she told herself. But she knew it was sheer denial. She was just trying to give her guilt a way out.

Qana was distraught. She has killed one sister already, and now she was about to kill the second.

⌐

Beirut—Tuesday, September 14, 1982

"I dare you to swallow that needle."

It was all those eyes' fault. Those flaming amber-green eyes. Everyone in Marwahin was in awe of them. Of everything in her and about her.

"Wow! What gorgeous chestnut hair she has!"

"How come you called her Fatima?"

"She sounds so cute when she speaks Armenian."

She had learned Armenian long before I did, even though she was two years younger than me. We almost had the same height. She was tall for her age, and I was short for mine. Our mother would sew us identical dresses, but we never looked like twins. Fatima was the "pretty" one.

"Can your daughter be the flower girl at my son's wedding? The pretty one?" I overheard the neighbor, Oum Raja, asking my mother. They didn't know that I was in the other room. "Both my daughters are pretty," Mother replied aggressively.

Thank you, Mama. But the neighbor is right. Look at me. I have plain black hair and plain black eyes. My skin is the color of a bread crust, while hers is milky.

"Wow! What A unique translucent complexion she has!"

Fatima was undeniably the pretty one. Which could only mean I was the ugly one.

I once heard that children of true love are born remarkably attractive. The more passionate the feelings between the parents at the moment of conception, the more beautiful the baby.

Was Mother more in love with Father when she got pregnant with Fatima? But it doesn't make any sense. I am the eldest: Love withers with time; it doesn't become stronger.

I'm in the perfect position to know that.

Fatima was Father's favorite one, too. I could feel it, even though he always tried to hide it. Whenever he came home from his work in the fields, she was the one he picked up and kissed first. When she was around, I'd become invisible.

"I dare you to swallow that needle."

It was her birthday and Mother had baked her a big cake. Bigger than the one she had baked for my birthday last March. I only wanted to hurt her a little bit, just like her existence was hurting me. I didn't know that she'd die. I swear I did not know.

That needle has been implanted in my heart ever since.

And today, it was Najat's turn. Another assassination. One more deadly needle.

But there was no other way. Luqa wouldn't let her stay at our house. Sorry, at "his" house.

"Why can't she live with us?" Qadar kept asking me when we left the hospital. What could I say? "Because your father is a selfish prick?" She wouldn't have believed me anyway. She adores him. He is her favorite.

Will I ever be someone's favorite?

⌐

Qana Barakat was born on a pleasant March morning of the year 1946. The cherry trees were starting to blossom in Deir

Yassin, and the whole of Jerusalem and the hills around it were in celebration mode.

The baby girl should have been called Fatima. Her parents had been married for thirteen years by the time her mother got pregnant with her. It was no less than a miracle, her father told her one day—even though she never felt special like a "miracle" should feel. An old woman had predicted her birth and insisted that her mother, Qayah, call the baby Fatima. But her father refused. They had to call her younger sister that name though, to lift some kind of a curse that fallen upon Qana because they hadn't abided by the fortune teller's request.

Had the curse really been lifted? Qana's later years kept insinuating to her that it had not. Often she'd remember that story, every time she'd see her life changing course before her eyes, for the worse, evidently. There didn't seem to be any other direction. Her Earth was not round; there weren't any circular roads. The only way was down. And no matter how hard she'd bustle and wrestle like a drowning cat in a pool, trying to plant her nails in one of the bordering walls, she'd keep on sliding.

Qana had always had to suffer in order to achieve or experience what other people consider normal or easy. She had a constant sense of being a load, of being one person too many in everybody's life.

⟵

Her father, Bassem, was a Melkite from Jerusalem, Palestine, and her mother Qayah was an Armenian, originally from Southeastern Turkey.

Qana had a deep sense of loyalty to Palestine. Not the emotional kind, but the ethical, which was as legitimate. She also identified a lot with her Armenian mother's identity and heritage, and spoke Armenian fluently, even though she had learned it rather late. It was, in this case too, more of a moral identification. A tribute to her mother.

For a long time, she did not suspect that there was such a dark past in her mother's life. She saw it, rather she felt it, that bottomless abyss in Qayah's soul. But she didn't know what had dug it. She only knew that Qayah was born in 1912, in a small town called Aintab where some war had broken out, and that she and her father Bassem had met in Jerusalem in 1930. The time between the two points was a blank space that she did not feel compelled to fill, not until late in her teens.

Eighteen mysterious years.

One day she would call them "the lost years of Qayah," like "the lost years of Jesus."

She asked herself many other questions though, while growing up. Despite her Palestinian and Armenian principled allegiances, Qana developed a strong sense of rootlessness, and had the existential interrogations of a child who feels out of place everywhere. Who/what was she? She was a home-sick kid without a home. It wasn't a poetic alienation, the one some people embrace by choice. In her self-image, despite her Lebanese identity card, she never really felt Lebanese.

She was a refugee and a descendent of serial refugees. "Refugee" is first and foremost a state of the mind rather than a situation. Few refugees have the opportunity or the nerve to truly blend in and identify with the host country. Integration requires a certain degree of audacity, insolence even, towards the natives. "I am as entitled as you!" The intrinsic fear of rejection, as well as the lack of prospects, can make refugees coagulate together and form separate communities, often disconnected from the locals.

Qana lived in Beirut ever since she was eight. But she was told that she was born in a village near Jerusalem, called Deir Yassin. She had no recollection whatsoever of that period in her life. Her parents had fled to Marwahin, in Southern Lebanon, immediately after the start of the Arab-Israeli war, and she was merely two years old then.

Marwahin: That place, she remembered very well on the other hand.

How could she forget?

↩

Marwahin—Friday, March 21, 1952

I can watch the ants for hours. They amaze me. They never stop moving, never stop working, never show any signs of exhaustion. Do they even sleep?

When I grow up, I want to be like an ant. I will work incessantly and do important things.

Today is the first day of spring, and I am wearing my new red skirt. It has two pockets, one on each side, and I have filled them with tiny pebbles which I tossed behind me on my way here into the woods. This way I will easily find my way back home. Just like Little Thumb, Al-Ossaybe'h,did. Father told me the story yesterday.

"Are there really ghouls out there, Baba?"

"No, my love. It's just a fairy tale. Fairy tales aren't real."

Mother had sewn me the red skirt for my sixth birthday. She also sewed one for Fatima. Our old neighbor, Jeddo, Grandpa, Ameen, came and sat on a rock by my side. How did he find me here? He must have followed the pebbles. He gave me a lollipop. He always gives me lollipops. He is such a nice man, Jeddo Ameen.

"Hello, ya ammoura, sweetie!"[39]

"Hello, Jeddo!"

"Is this skirt new? It looks so nice on you!"

"Yes. Mama sewed one for me and one for Fatima. But it looks

....

39 Lebanese, literally "small moon."

a lot better on Fatima."

"That's not true! I just saw Fatima on my way here, and it doesn't look that good on her."

I was sucking the lollipop. The flavor was strawberry, my favorite. I felt delighted.

"Really?"

"Of course! I would never lie to you. What are you doing here?"

"I came to watch the ants! There aren't enough near our house, and whenever I find some, Mother pours Kerosene on them and they die. I love ants. Aren't they amazing?"

"They sure are. Tell you what. I will build the most impressive ant farm for you, just like the one I've built for Youssef."

"Oh! Thank you so much Jeddo! I love ant farms. I've always dreamed of having one ever since Youssef has showed me his!"

Youssef was Jeddo Ameen's grandson. He wouldn't let me anywhere near his ant farm. He only showed it to me to tease me. He was mean.

"You're welcome! I will make it even bigger than Youssef's. But I need one thing from you in return. Would you do it for me?"

"Of course! Anything!"

He took out a black scarf from his pocket.

"We are going to play a game. It's actually a very fun game. I'm going to cover your eyes with this scarf. Then you are going to kneel down and I am going to put something in your mouth and you will lick it and suck it. Just like you are sucking the lollipop now."

I got nervous.

"Why should I have my eyes covered, Jeddo?"

"Because that's the rule of the game. Just like hide and seek."

I loved playing hide and seek. I was very good at it too.

"Will that thing taste bad?"

"Not at all. You might find it a bit strange at first. But you will soon like it."

...

◇ ♡ ♠ ♧

I didn't like it at all. It felt slimy in my mouth, like the snails that Mother cooks for us after the first rainfall, and I hated snails. It also smelled bad. But I said nothing because I didn't want to upset Jeddo Ameen. He was going to build me an ant farm! Bigger than Youssef's!

Then he started breathing raucously. I got scared and stopped.

"Jeddo, are you all right?"

He pushed the snail back in my mouth. I almost choked.

"Yes, yes, continue!"

His voice was so weird. Transformed.

The snail was becoming bigger, and I was starting to find it hard to breathe. Then it spat a bitter liquid on my tongue.

"Swallow, swallow!"

So I swallowed. My throat and stomach were burning, but I swallowed. I felt like throwing up but I swallowed. I didn't want to upset Jeddo. He was going to build me an ant farm!

Luckily it was soon over after that. He took the scarf off my eyes and I stood up. "Good girl" he said, and he patted me on the head. He gave me another lollipop. I was proud. He chose me to play the game, not Fatima.

"Don't tell your parents about this! Don't you dare! It is our secret."

"OK."

I felt special. I felt like a grown-up. Only grown-ups have secrets.

We kept on playing this game, and other ones too, until the day we left Marwahin: September 11, 1954. I remember the date very well because as the taxi drove us away, I finally stopped feeling dirty and ashamed.

Jeddo Ameen never built me an ant farm.

Baba, you were wrong. Ghouls are real.

—

Qana was the only student in Bourj Hammoud's Armenian Elementary School with an Arabic sounding name. Yet she did speak Armenian—rather poorly at first then soon with ease—which made her an exception. The kids didn't like exceptions. Most of them were taught to feel threatened by anything or anyone that stood out, and to unite against it/them.

"Kill the impudent drifter," say the bleating, head-sagging sheep. "The flock is sacred."

But it's not the flock they are guarding. It's their fear.

"*Spasuhiyin aghjike*, the maid's daughter, they called Qana, especially the girls, to humiliate her. She had a unique gift for making other girls feel madly jealous and becoming obnoxious bullies, even the nicest ones. And she actually relished their jealousy. She fed on it like a vampire and got her validation from it. To her, the forever invisible previous her, it was an affirmation of being. It didn't help that the more she blossomed, the more attention she got from the boys.

Qana was stunning, and grew up unaware of being so, which made her even more stunning. She had blue-black silky hair, dark eyes that could eat you alive, and golden brown skin. She wasn't tall, rather on the petite side, but what she lacked in height, she compensated for in magnetism. Her charisma made her look like a giant. As a child, she always thought she was plain, so she unconsciously cultivated all of her feminine behavioral and scheming assets to perfection, to make up for her self-presumed unattractiveness. The result was dangerous: a female creature who, already at the teen stage, was both Eve and the Snake. The promising rough sketch of a future "femme fatale." She was also an early bloomer, not only psychologically because she had been abused as a kid, but also physically. At the age of twelve she looked seventeen. Her body was fully armed and ready for war. She was a broken hearts collector, like all ugly ducklings, and broken hearts she collected indeed, a whole lot of them. But she would never feel satisfied. She couldn't. More, she constantly wanted more—more attention, more admiration, more homages and more despairs, so that she could feel avenged. "How do you see me now, Oum Raja?"

"Spasuhiyin aghjike! Spasuhiyin aghjike!"

"Shut up!"

This maid's daughter was no dove. Qana couldn't be forgiving or lenient, even if she wanted to. Anger lived inside her as if it were at home, and she was good at it. She would beat them up one by one. She would beat them for way more than what they were saying or doing.

"My mother is a seamstress, not a maid!"

Not that the seamstress' profession indicated a much higher social rank. Still, anything for Qana was better than the submissive, "servant" label. Anything was better than getting down on all fours and mopping toilets. But her mother would regularly appear during recess with a bucket of water, a bar of soap, and a brush, and Qana, mortified, would wish she could just disappear.

"Why don't you go back to sewing like you used to when I was a kid?" So many times she wanted to make that suggestion to Qayah, but she never dared. She knew very well why her mother had stopped being a seamstress. It was her own fault. However, she fervently wished that Qayah didn't have to clean her school. Out of all the places where she could work in Beirut, did she have to pick that one? Qana didn't know that she could study in that private institution only because her mother was going down on her hands and knees there every day. Qayah never told her.

The continuous, violent confrontations she had with her schoolmates, which gained her the nickname "*Gazan*"—"Beast," didn't last for long, though. Qana had to leave school and get a job in a nearby clothing factory immediately after receiving her Elementary Certificate in June 1960, with rudimentary knowledge in Arabic and Armenian. She was fourteen already and she had to help her parents. Only a few months ago, they had found out that her sister Najat was seriously ill.

Qana enjoyed sewing and was very good at it. She had learned to do it by herself on the old Singer machine of the next door neighbor Elham. Ever since she was twelve she started sewing her own clothes. With very humble means and materials, she managed to turn heads. Not only men's but women's, as well, which was a bigger challenge.

What she wore was always different—unique and inventive. Very soon, however, she hated the clothing factory and her job there. It was a soulless, repetitive job. There were dozens of other girls like her, and they would all be operating like robots from eight to five, each group doing a specific chore. She was part of the group that sewed hems, nothing but hems all day long.

She had dreamed of inspiration and glamour, and the factory was anything but inspirational and glamorous. However, she did what had to be done and lived what had to be lived. "Remember the ants, Qana!" she would tell herself when her fingers and her back would become too sore after long hours at the machine. She was paid by the piece. The more pieces she got done, the more money she took home, which forced her to race with the hours. She was already the opposite of sluggish, but the impetus of the "extra cash" made her work at a frenzied pace. It was nerve wrecking. If it weren't for the insistence of one caring co-worker, "Somaya the Palestinian," as the chief atelier called her, she wouldn't take any breaks.

Man against Time, David against Goliath—with a totally different ending to the story. A more realistic one. Because even if you defeat the Giant temporarily, you will still be the loser in the game. Lightness is no trivial loss for a human being. And how could anyone who's been trained to run marathons so early in life, ever be able to feel light? To slow down and live the moment?

Stitch, stitch, stitch. Stitch away your wounds, little girl with the red skirt. Stitch and try to forget that needle piercing your memory like a pointed finger.

And never mind the pebbles. Whatever you do, you'll never find your way back home.

〜

Bourj Hammoud—Monday, February 20, 1961

I saw him again this morning. We bumped into each other on the stairs. I was heading to the factory, and he was on his way to open his father's laundry. I don't think it was an accident, because this is the fourth day in a row that the same "accident" has occurred. I'm almost sure he has calculated my timing and was lurking somewhere upstairs. As soon as I opened our apartment door and got out, I could hear his steps running down. He passed by me, stopped, turned around and stood in my way.

"Good morning," he said to me, smiling. "Will you finally tell me your name, Anisa[40] Qana?

I laughed. He must have asked one of the neighbors.

"Not until you tell me yours, Myouqra[41] Luqa!"

His eyes lit up. I gave him the boost deliberately. I usually like to tease the boys. I love ignoring and snubbing them until they lose their minds and become ripe. Soft under the machete. But this one

....

40   Arabic for "miss"
41   Assyrian for "mister."

153

was different. This one, I decided, deserved a crumb of reassurance earlier than the others.

"I wrote you something yesterday."

He gave me a folded paper.

"What is it?"

"A poem. But I doubt it is worthy of your majesty."

He was stroking the right spot: my ego.

I'd already seen him a few times during the past three years, sitting behind the counter at his father's shop, reading. He was always so taken by the book in his hands that he never noticed me, not even once. It annoyed me. But as soon as he laid eyes on me, the day he was carrying boxes up, helping his family move into the building, I could immediately tell he wasn't going to forget me.

I know how to read squints. His was clearly saying, "I'm ruined."

He most certainly was.

He always looked so mysterious and appealing. Mature also. Way more mature than the teenagers that kept stalking me. I never saw him wearing shorts. He always had a white shirt and black trousers on.

"I'll read it. Goodbye now. I'm late for work."

"Wait. Before you go..."

"Yes?"

"Do I have to keep running into you, or can we start meeting on purpose?"

"He's already had his dose of encouragement for the day. No need to go crazy and give him more. He'll have to deserve it," Qana the Snake whispered in the ear of Qana the Eve.

"I'll think about it," I said.

Then, as I was exiting the building: "Meanwhile, keep the coincidences happening."

I smiled saying that. My smile was addictive. The most powerful of baits. But I didn't need any. He was already hooked.

Once her utilitarian labor deprived Qana of the creative joy she used to feel when sewing, the memory of Fatima returned. The memory of what she had done to her. Before then, she had somehow managed to bury the incident under layers of denial and fake distractions, but one day, it resurged with full force, and she could do nothing to fight it anymore. Traumas always do that. Sometimes Qana would pierce herself with the needles on purpose. Her arms, hands, thighs. She wouldn't settle for a light puncture or a thin needle. She'd choose the thickest ones, with the sharpest tips. She had to feel the burn, see the blood come out, the regrets drip down. As if she was temporarily clearing her clogged memory.

What is the use of regret? Aren't most mistakes beyond redemption? We fool ourselves with the literature of remorse and recuperation. But truth is that a culpable conscience will keep on beating like a drum in our heads, at all the wrong times and in all the wrong places.

That is one of the reasons why what has died is more enviable than what still has to die.

Qana was immersed in her gloomy thoughts one day when, right out of the blue, amidst all the anger and bleakness, she smiled, a strange smile that rose like a wild purple flower among ruins. She did not smile because she was slowly becoming insane. Nor did she smile because her heart was turning into stone. (How she wished it did, at times.) She smiled because she remembered Luqa. She had a feeling he was the one. The one she's been waiting for. The one that could make all of *this* disappear. This: the factory's dirty windows. Her mother's imploding grief. Her father's soaring exhaustion. Her sister's hollow eyes. Her own impervious anxieties. Her poisonous memories. And her inability to manufacture joy.

She went back to her book, the one Luqa had given her to read last week, *Al-Ragheef* [42] by Toufik Youssef Awwad. It wasn't as difficult as she thought it would be. She had decided to improve her Arabic for his sake, as he was passionate about the language, and she wanted to grasp all the meanings that his letters conveyed. But her strenuous job never allowed her to follow any discipline. That was so like her: gifted for interruption, incomplete endeavors. It was almost a miracle she wasn't born missing a liver or a leg...

Luqa had promised to give her private lessons: "I insist on teaching you," he said. Soon he would be arriving at her house for their daily evening class, and she was impatiently waiting for him on the balcony, trying to detect the sound of the steel roller door of the shop below being closed.

"Wa lakinnakom la takhafun al mawt, bal antum takhafun al hayat: But you are not afraid of death; you are afraid of life."[43]

＊

Bourj Hammoud—Friday, January 24, 1964

There has to be a first time. Always.

The first time our innocence is scratched. The first time our heart closes in on us like a mouse trap. The first time we taste sourness. The first time we opt for silence. The first time we discover endings. The first time we are forced to understand what we did not want to understand. The first time we open our eyes and really see the world. Its incongruity, its capriciousness. The rawness of its beauty. The grandeur of its primitiveness.

There has to be a first time. Always.

.........The first time we realize that every road ahead is an impasse.

42 Arabic for "The Loaf of Bread." This 1939 classic Lebanese novel revolves around Lebanon and the Arab world during World War I.

43 From Al-Ragheef.

◇ ♡ ♠ ♣

⌐

The first time Qana really saw her own mother Qayah, it was with Luqa's eyes. Rather, with his words. Neither her mother nor Luqa's parents ever discussed with their children their pasts in Turkey. But he had heard many stories from his Mardini tutor about what had happened to the Armenians and to other Christian minorities like his own family in 1915. So one evening, while they were sipping soda in one of Rawcheh's cafés, he shared them with her. It was February 1st, 1964, one month before her eighteenth birthday, the date on which he was planning to propose to her, and he wanted to make sure she'd say yes. He intuited the knowledge would draw her closer to him.

Qana was incredulous at first.

"This can't be right."

She already knew there had been a war. But this was too much. Too much horror. Too much pain. Too much everything.

"Your tutor must have been exaggerating."

But then she went home and asked Qayah a question. Then a second one, and a third. Her mother's reaction was silence. Utter silence so loud it was deafening. A silence that could only mean one thing: that what Luqa had told her was true.

The following days, Qana kept questioning her mother about that chapter in her life. "Why did you leave Aintab?" "How come you went to Jerusalem?" "What happened to your parents?" "Do you have any brothers and sisters?" "How was your life before you met Baba?"

Nothing. As if these questions were larger than Qayah. As if the eighteen mysterious years had never existed in her life.

Or over-existed.

Qana kept trying. Up until a point when, watching her mother sink into an abysmal melancholy, she decided to stop. She did manage to get some answers from Bassem who, weirdly, didn't know much, but still knew more than she did: That Qayah was an orphan who lost her family in Turkey during the genocide. That she had been adopted by an Armenian couple in Aleppo. That the couple had moved to Jerusalem when Qayah was eight years old. That Qayah's adoptive mother was a skilled seamstress called Vartouhi, and that her biological mother had been a seamstress, too. That Qayah's best friend in Jerusalem was called Negan, which means "destiny" in Persian, and that Bassem had met her through Negan's father, Shafik, who was one of his own dearest friends.

Most of this information came actually from Shafik, Bassem told Qana, who in turn had gotten it from Vartouhi. Qayah never spoke to him about her past. He knew nothing about any siblings she might have had, but he did know, from her identity card, that her original parents' names were Nazar and Marine. That was all.

So many earthquakes in so few words.

Luqa's hunch was right. The immeasurable discovery increased Qana's complicity with him. The fact that her mother and his parents shared the same suffering was seen by her as a sign. She and Luqa were united by tragedy. A tragedy that she intuited was darker than they both could ever imagine, which reinforced her superstition that they were meant for each other. The only thing that they didn't have in common was their perception of Lebanon: Qana never felt any real belonging to it, while Luqa had unwavering national Lebanese fervor. He grew up with an almost fanatic loyalty to the idea of Lebanon.

That's what Lebanon was, is, and will always be at best: an idea.

A great one though.

In March of 1964, Luqa proposed to Qana. But a series of deaths in his family, starting with his father's, kept forcing them to postpone their wedding date. The Assyrians took mourning very seriously. His poems and passionate love letters kept on coming though, for many following years. When they finally did get married on March 2, 1969, Qana had six hundred and twenty-four letters from Luqa. Six hundred and twenty-four promises of undying adoration. The neighbors had nicknamed them the building's Qais and Layla, famous Arab lovers, the Romeo and Juliet of the Desert. They even had the same initials, Q and L, though inverted.

The lovebirds did the math: Their two families combined had witnessed the 1914 First World War, the 1915 Armenian and Assyrian genocides, the 1939 second World War, the 1948 Arab-Israeli war and the 1958 Lebanon crisis. Wars, inside and outside, would keep on tying them together endlessly, growing and snaking around them, between them, under their feet, above their heads and around their necks like wild plants in the Amazon forest.

No bond is stronger than sorrow. And none more volatile, more easily transformable into aversion. Too much of seeing your own torment in another other person's face can, *will*, make you eventually hate them. We think we need to be reminded of who we are in order to survive, but what we often need is to forget it. To emancipate ourselves from it. To shed it like a wrinkly craggy skin and start anew.

Life requires the skill of tirelessly beginning ourselves again. Love, too.

It was no writer's whim: Qais and Layla simply had to die.

⌒

Bourj Hammoud—Thursday, September 24, 1970

She has Mother's red curls. Pure, deep, flaming red curls. The doctor told me he's never seen an infant with so much hair. He also said that she was born with her eyes wide open. Very unusual, he observed.

"Is that good or bad?"

"Neither. Just rare."

I will call her Qadar. Like Mother's best friend back in Jerusalem, only in Arabic. Her name is bound to draw her good luck. Qadar will be smart and pretty. Not my kind of pretty. Much prettier. No one will ever make fun of her or shame her. I won't let that happen. She will be ambitious and hardworking, and she will achieve wonderful things. Things like what newspapers write about.

She will be a courageous lawyer defending the innocent. No, a remarkable doctor saving people's lives. No, a brilliant engineer building huge edifices…Can she become an astronaut? I heard that a man, an American, traveled to the moon last year. To the moon! They said he was an astronaut. Maybe my Qadar will also travel to the moon one day. Why not? Anything is possible. I will make it possible.

Or maybe she'll be a fashion designer. What I have always dreamed to be. A very talented and renowned one, like Coco Chanel. She will have clothes in her name, and perfumes too. There was a poster of Coco Chanel on one of the factory's walls. In it we see her wearing a black dress and a pearl necklace. Smiling but not too much, just like rich, self-confident people smile. They only smile a little because they can. Because when you have money you don't need to prove to others that you are happy. They know. And you know.

I used to look at that poster every day and think: "What an elegant, poised woman!" I did not realize who she was then. There was no name on the poster. I thought she was the boss' mother or something: Then one day I saw the same photo in a fashion magazine, with a name written in bold letters. "Mademoiselle Coco Chanel." That's when I read the story of her struggle and fell in love with her.

She was born extremely poor and had a difficult life. She was taught how to sew in the orphanage where she grew up. But she didn't let any obstacle stand between her and what she wanted. She worked her way up from literally nothing to become one of the most celebrated designers in the history of fashion. In the interview she says, "My life didn't please me, so I created my life."

I wish I could have created mine.

Willpower is not always enough, Mademoiselle Coco. One needs a nudge from providence. Like a rich lover.

But that's what my Qadar will do. She will create her life. She will be famous and successful. She will meet lots of interesting people, and one day, when the time comes, she will marry someone who appreciates her and knows her worth. Someone who will look after her and let her have no worries. No worries whatsoever.

Qadar will travel too. I've always dreamed of traveling. One of Luqa's cousins works as a hostess at Middle East Airlines, and she is constantly visiting these splendid places. She described Paris to me. Apparently there's a tower there so high that you can see it from a very remote place. Mariam also told me that Paris is the city of love. Romantic and magical, she said. I would love to see Paris one day. That's where Coco Chanel lives. Maybe when Qadar becomes famous and successful she'll take me there.

Luqa has promised to take me, but something is telling me he won't.

⟶

"I promise I will always look after you. Always."

And Qana believed him. She needed to. But soon after their marriage, she discovered that his promises were nothing but obsolete currencies. Every time he'd make a new promise to her she'd cynically ask him, "*Wayn bosrofa hayde,* where can I spend this one?"[44]

Every time she'd tell him about a bill to pay, a house appliance to repair (never to "replace," that was out of the

....

44   A Lebanese way of telling someone that their promise is BS.

question), an urgent purchase for their daughter, he'd take his eyes off his precious book for a second and say, "I promise I'll find a solution soon. Stop stressing."

Paying up a promise with another promise.

"Find a solution where, Luqa. In Ibn Khaldun's *Prolegomena*?"

"If I stopped stressing, we'd be starving."

Life was getting tough, especially since the start of the war. The laundry was hardly thriving before, with Luqa's continuous delivery delays and unforgivable sloppiness, which alienated the clients that his father had diligently gathered over the years. But after 1975, the situation became even worse, and the few remaining loyal customers disappeared one after the other. Who bothers about wrinkled shirts when people are dying? They had decided to send Qadar to a rather expensive private school, and it took Qana a lot of effort and sacrifice to be able to pay her tuition. She couldn't even remember when she had last bought something for herself, except for the monthly fashion magazine, her only "vice." A vice that helped her keep her secret dream alive and forget that she'd been wearing the same clothes for years. She didn't mind. She wasn't interested in new dresses, fancy jewelry, high-quality makeup, or sophisticated hairdos. Her daughter's future was the only thing she wouldn't compromise on. One day Qadar will become what Qana couldn't be. What Qana could have been, only if.

Only if. Qana was a realist. She knew that it was useless to contemplate the ways in which a life, any life, would have been different "if." "Ifs" were strictly reserved for people with money; people who can afford tryouts; people who grow up fearless because they know that they can flop and start again; people, first and foremost, who've never had to supplicate for anything.

Qana will never forget the day when, after the war began

and their financial situation deteriorated, she went to Qadar's school to ask for a tuition reduction. The nuns had taken the girl out of her class the day before, and made her sit on the stairs like some beggar, because her parents still hadn't paid all of her school fees. Qana would endure anything for her daughter not to be demeaned like that again in front of her classmates. She kneeled down in front of *Soeur* Constance, crying and imploring her. But no matter how much she prayed, the merciless nun wouldn't grant her any discount. "Why don't you transfer her to a public school?"

It was a hard blow to Qana's pride. She was not a woman to show weakness or need, even when she felt them or when life made her feel them, which was often. One time, when Qadar had drunk the whole glass of rosewater at the neighbor's house, she slapped her hard once they got back home.

"You always leave some behind. Always! Now they will think that we are not providing for you."

Like many poor people, she had a lot of amour propre in her, self-worth, arrogance even. Her dignity was sacred material. So she started depriving herself to make ends meet. But never did she let her daughter notice any of it.

"Why aren't you drinking milk anymore Mama?" Qadar would ask her while savoring her daily morning glass of Nido powdered milk.

"I just don't like it anymore."

"Can I please have one more glass?"

"No. One is enough, or you will have stomach ache."

Qadar adored milk. Long after Qana had started giving her solid food, she would still demand her everyday morning and evening bottles.

"Why don't you transfer her to a public school?"

Yeah. That's exactly what Jesus would have said, *Soeur* Constance.

↙

Bourj Hammoud—Sunday, June 6, 1976

Sunday is my father's only day off. He still works hard, even though he is eighty-two. Mother had to give up sewing because her hands can't stop shaking now, and her sight has become very faint. Najat needs Valium. Lots and lots of it. And Valium is not cheap. I do chip in, but I wish I could help them more. They don't know it, but my own situation is difficult enough. Last week I had to use some of the safety money to cover Qadar's tuition. I also sold my engagement ring. I didn't have to, not just yet. But I really wanted to. It was a reminder of the time when I was gullible and stupid.

Luqa spends most of his time at the laundry reading books. I keep asking him to get out there and look for a job, but he won't listen. Reading is all he's good at. That, and coming up with pretentious judgments about life. A know-it-all, that's what he is. Books don't appease hunger, Istez.[45] Books don't pay schools' tuitions.

Get up, move, do something!

We went to have lunch at my mother's today. She had cooked Luqa's favorite Armenian dish: manteh. She admires him and likes to please him. Not that he deserves it. She thinks highly of him only because he's well read, and I never complain to her about our marriage. Whenever she asks me how things are, I keep telling her, "Hamdella, thank God!"

She doesn't need any more worries.

The radio was on like it's continually been in every Lebanese household since the start of the war. As we were about to finish eating, we heard in the news bulletin a virulent statement by Bachir Gemayel. Five days earlier, the Syrian troops had officially entered Lebanon to help the Christians put an end to the ongoing war. In his

....

45   Arabic for "Mister."

statement, Gemayel protested the Syrian intervention, and has even threatened to submit his resignation from his party, the Kata'eb,[46] *because the latter has approved the entrance of the Syrian Army.*

"Now that's a true hero!" Luqa exclaimed as soon as Gemayel's statement was over.

"He's just an assassin!" I protested.

I couldn't let him get away with such bullshit, even if I had to argue with him in front of Mother and Qadar, which I had promised myself not to do. But I abhor this Gemayel. He has slaughtered so many Palestinians. I lost my dear friend Somaya last January. The kind, affectionate Somaya. As soon as they found out she was Palestinian from her accent, the Phalanges shot her near her house in Karantina, while she was on her way to buy bread. When I heard the news, I felt like tearing up my Lebanese identity card. One month before that, the same Phalanges had committed another massacre against the Palestinians, on a day so horrible that it got called the "Black Saturday."

Criminals, all of them. The leaders quarrel and the innocent die.

But Luqa wouldn't shut up.

"Never call him an assassin again! The real assassins are your kind!"

"My kind?" I got goosebumps from all the fury I felt. It wasn't just the two words. It was his tone when he said them—condescending, haughty, offensive. He was taking advantage of Father's absence to attack the Palestinians.

"Really? Then you should welcome the Syrians with open arms. Aren't they coming to help you against 'my kind'?"

"Stop blabbering about things you know nothing about. This is politics. The Syrians want to take over Lebanon. All this talk about helping the Christians is a lie."

Mother took his side. I already knew she held a grudge against

....

46   The Lebanese Phalanges.

the Palestinians. A fierce one. She never told me why though. And not once did she express this resentment of hers in front of Father. She protected his feelings.

I didn't give a damn about politics or the Syrians or the Christians. I didn't give a damn about Lebanon either. It was just another place and places don't matter.

Only people do. People who die while buying bread for their families.

People who don't sit down and read while their wives go down on their knees, Luqa.

⌒

"*Kaniyeh*, how much is it?" she asked in Armenian, dreading the answer. The shop was too fancy.

"Sixty liras," the saleswoman replied in a dry tone, looking at her rather disdainfully as if implying, "This is clearly above your means."

Luqa now barely earned two hundred liras a month. Qana stood there, first staring at the dress, then examining it up close. It was white piqué, with blue embroidery on the sleeves and the hem.

"Anything else?" the saleswoman asked her snappishly.

Meaning: "Shoo now."

Qana dragged an inconsolable Qadar out of the shop.

"I'll make you an even nicer one."

Ever since she was six, Qadar seemed only to be interested in two things: good books and nice clothes. How did she combine the two interests, the two appetites, Qana never understood. She always thought that they were mutually exclusive. That the bookish girls didn't care about looks, and the stylish girls didn't care about books. Qadar proved her wrong. As if the girl was a perfect mathematical equation: the exact sum of half her mother and half her father. Fortunately, Luqa had a lot of books ("too many," Qana would mumble with a grudge while dusting the wooden shelves), and he always managed to get more and more from his acquaintances. But her daughter's premature passion for fashion, on the other hand, was turning out to be quite costly.

"What am I going to wear to Dodo's birthday party?"

"How about that purple dress I got you from the boutique last summer?"

"No way! I already wore it to Tima's wedding and everyone has seen me in it!"

She was seven, for heaven's sake! How can a seven-year-old-girl be so coquettish? And she knew her subject. What goes with what, which prints were fashionable each season, how a certain pattern would suit a particular body and not another, and, of course, what colors should a redhead avoid! Every month she'd browse *Burda*'s newest issue, even before her mother did.

Qana had quit her job at the clothing factory when she and Luqa got married. After nine years of what she referred to as "slavery," she kept having frequent nightmares about that place, long after she had left it. The most recurring was one where the sewing machines would turn into gigantic ants and eat her alive. But now she wished she hadn't quit. She had to find a solution, and fast.

She had managed to put some cash aside from the time when she worked, but she reserved it for strict emergencies. She used to finish twenty-two pieces a day, sometimes even more, while the other girls delivered an average of fifteen or sixteen. She'd give her mother the pay she'd gotten for twenty, and hide the rest. "Save your white piaster for your black day."

Qana saved and saved. She couldn't squander money even if she wanted to. The result was a modest fortune of 1,170 liras: 260 working days a year, with two pieces' pay saved every day, 25 *oirshs*[47] for the piece, during nine years. She called it her safety money and kept it in a small black leather bag hidden in her daughter's closet. She had already used some of it to cover the deficit in Qadar's school fees along the years. She never told Luqa about it, not even before they got married. Something kept warning her not to. And she'd certainly not tell him about it now. He didn't need more excuses to relax, sit down, and do nothing.

She had noticed the sewing machine before. It was displayed in Baron Hagop's shop window. A used Mercedes. It seemed like the perfect solution. *I could buy it using some of the safety money*, she reasoned. *This way I could make some extra cash for Qadar's education, and I could sew her all the dresses she wants, as well.*

So she bought it. She also bought threads of all colors, a measuring tape, a good pair of scissors, needles and pins, an assortment of buttons, a marking tool and a thimble. She didn't forget to add two meters of white piqué, the best that Baron Hagop had, and one roll of a special blue thread, exclusively fabricated for embroidery. Viscose, not polyester.

"I'll make you an even nicer one."

While carrying the Mercedes sewing machine back home that day, Qana was smiling and thinking: "Now my Qadar can also have two glasses of milk each morning."

⌐

Beirut—Tuesday, April 11, 1978

I knew she was going to do it. Ever since she sat me down yesterday and told me all the darknesses that were long left untold between us. The eighteen lost years of Qayah are no longer lost.

I knew she was going to do it. Ever since she gave Qadar her

....

47   Old coin currency in Lebanon.

locket, the only treasure that she had. The steel locket between Qadar's playful little hands started resonating. Ding. Ding. Ding. It sounded like a farewell bell ring. A soft, barely audible goodbye.

Now I will have to walk alone with her ghosts. And I can't look back because she closed the door behind me. Behind us.

How ready are we to become the owners of another person's tears? Often we ask questions that we don't really want answered. The questions relieve us. "We tried." But every once in a while, the answers do come, unexpected. The rain starts falling, more rain than our eyes could ever absorb, and we feel overwhelmed by the certainty that we can never become innocent again.

I used to think that in order to live, we need to be quick. Quick enough to receive the ball the world keeps kicking at us and swiftly boot it away again. Now I know that we need to pretend we didn't see the ball. Or else the game would never end until the day we die.

I knew she was going to do it. She always had that confounded expression in her eyes. An expression that meant: I do not belong here.

Now that you are gone, Mayrik, tell me: Do we ever belong anywhere?

She hated herself, more and more every day, but she couldn't help it. It was as if she was possessed by a demon. And it was the demon who would beat up her daughter, not her. Then she'd come back from her stupor and realize what she had done. No. Not *her*: what the *demon* had done. She would never consciously do something so hideous. Qadar was her life.

There were voices in Qana's head. Voices screaming all the time. Screaming awful things. That she was a bad mother. A bad daughter. A bad wife. Voices making her feel hopeless. Sad. Irritable. Angry. Aggressive. Voices pushing her to keep cleaning. Everything is dirty, Qana! Wash! Rub! Mop! Brush! Dust! Wipe! Voices, also, telling her to hit her daughter. She went to a doctor once. At first he thought she was schizo-phrenic. Then after endless interrogations, he told her that she had obsessive compulsive disorder. "That's excellent!" he said, almost delighted. "Schizophrenia is way more complicated and threatening." Qana wondered, looking at the smile on his face, if she should celebrate because she "only" had OCD.

Apparently, it was the OCD that made her have repeated irrational and violent ideas, those she called "the voices." Apparently, the more she'd fight those ideas, the stronger they'd become. "But doctor, you don't understand, I nearly killed my daughter last Friday. I threw the ironing machine at her." He gave her pills. Qana did not want any pills. Pills had turned her sister into the living dead.

The doctor also recommended that she see a psychothera-pist. Overcoming the syndrome required analysis, counseling, patience and constant follow-up.

"You have to learn to fight the illogical with the tools of the logic."

It was a new habit that the therapist would help her acquire over time.

"It's the only real treatment for what is wrong with you," the doctor said.

—

Beirut—Monday, September 26, 1983

"Let me tell you what's really wrong with me, dear doctor!

"I am a failure. I am married to a failure. I was molested as a child. I killed my first sister. I jailed my second sister in a psychiatric hospital. My mother committed suicide. Two weeks ago, I lost the only man on the face of this earth who has really loved me. Last week, I discovered I was carrying his baby. This past Saturday, I murdered our baby. My daughter saw it all. I had to take her along

to help me get home. Now, she hates me, and I hate myself too. That's what's wrong with me."

I didn't say any of those things out loud to him. I only said them to myself as I was leaving his clinic. I threw the box of pills he had given me in a trashcan on the street.

A trashcan that looks a lot like my life.

⤙

It was the most difficult thing she'd ever had to do, but Qana knew she had to do it. For her daughter's sake, not hers. She didn't seek redemption; she only wanted to save Qadar from desiccation.

She had felt the recent change in her. Something big had happened in her life. Something extraordinary that had turned her into a softer, lighter version of herself. "It must be love." And Qadar should grab it and never let it go. Qana had been aware for a long time that her daughter's marriage was a fiasco. And today was a significant date; opportune for the confession she has been intent on making.

It was a cold winter morning in 2005. Qana was rushing to finish Qadar's favorite dish before her daughter's expected arrival at nine. *Adas b Hamod*, a comforting lentil soup cooked with chard and lemon. Qadar had been coming to Beirut a lot lately, but she never stayed at her parents' house. "I feel more comfortable in a hotel, Mother," she'd explain.

Qana wasted no time. As soon as Qadar came in and they sat down and were sipping their coffee, she set out.

"Today would have been our twenty-fifth anniversary."

Qadar looked at her mother, puzzled. Qana went on.

"He was kind and generous. He always sent us the best products from his grocery store for free. The basics and the extras. 'This chocolate is for Qadar'; 'Qadar would love this brand of ice-cream,'" he would say.

"You remember him, don't you? You used to pick up the goods from his shop sometimes. You wondered how come we didn't have to pay him, and I'd always tell you I had given him the money in advance.

"He really loved me Qadar. As I was. I was finally someone's favorite.

"They killed him. It was the 12th of September, 1983. The Druze had just massacred hundreds of Christian civilians and militia fighters in the Mountain War. In Bhamdoun, in Bireh, in Chartoun, and in so many other towns around Jabal. Throats cut, heads falling off like coconuts from palm trees. And the Christian militiamen retaliated of course. Khaldoun was a Druze. A Druze living in a Christian neighborhood. An easy duck. He had to be one of those bystanders who pay the price for their identity. I was told it was two of his store's clients who shot him. Antoine, whom he had known since he was five, and Elie, the son of the widow Oum Elie, whom Khaldoun always gave a discount.

"Oum Elie used to say to Khaldoun, '*Allah Yehmik, may God protect you!*' to express her gratitude.

"The day he was murdered, she danced in the street, and ululated.

Qana confessed everything to her daughter.

What came before and after. How little by little she had become encircled by cruelty. Jeddo Ameen and what he had done to little Qana. Fatima and what little Qana had done to her. The factory and how it killed her soul. Luqa and how he drained her aspirations. Qayah's revelations before suicide. Aintab. Adana. Jerusalem. Negan. Avi. And then Soeur Constance. And Najat. And losing love after finding love.

The exhaustion. The poverty. The responsibilities. The defeats...

All that weight, alone.

◇ ♡ ♠ ♧

"Don't waste your life like I did."

A newsflash on TV interrupted her. A famous Lebanese journalist's portrait appeared on the screen. Both Qana and Qadar reached for the remote.

A car bomb has just killed outspoken Lebanese journalist and anti-Syrian politician Gebran Tueni, a day after he had returned from Paris. At around 9 this morning, a booby-trapped Renault with up to 40 kg of dynamite was exploded by remote control in the Mkalles area, as Tueni's armored Range Rover drove by on the way to his office at the *An-Nahar* newspaper in downtown Beirut. Tueni, 48-year-old MP for the Orthodox seat in Ashrafieh, was accompanied by Andre Michel and by his driver Nicolas al-Flouti. All three died in the blast. The total number of the injured has yet to be confirmed. Tueni was a prominent opposition politician and was active in protests following Hariri's assassination. Those protests have helped prompt Syria to withdraw from Lebanon.

Another massive loss in this country's bloody history…

Qadar was crying. Both for her mother and for Gebran. But Qana hadn't finished. There was one more thing she still had to say. Maybe the hardest. Taking her daughter's hands in hers, she told her.

"The baby was a boy, Qadar."

⌐

Beirut—Monday, April 13, 2015

She is barely eating anymore. I must keep an eye on her and force her to swallow some food or she'll starve herself. She's not sleeping

173

either. Luqa and I can hear her moving around the house at night, flapping her limbs like a paper shadow. She does nothing all day. Just sits by the window with her hollow eyes, looking ahead. Rather, looking behind, at the trail of blood leading to her. The footsteps of death.

Are we using our time or not when we are wasting it away? Isn't waiting for an end also living? Life does not discriminate. It flows evenly in the heart that sings and in the heart that weeps.

Every now and then she'd try to scribble something on a piece of paper, holding the pen as if it were a shovel.

Her own gravedigger: that's what she's become.

Is that even possible?

Of course it is. All of us are.

Some are just more in a hurry than others. That is all the difference.

[4]

QAMAR

(Aleppo, 1997 –)

Great-granddaughter of Qayah
Granddaughter of Qana
Daughter of Qadar

"She who conquered the end and its beginnings"

♔

The **Queen of Clubs** has the sharp tongue that usually comes with a quarrelsome temper. She is impulsive, stubborn and outspoken, leaving others knowing exactly where they stand. Whatever she does, she cannot escape her past karmas. Her destiny is ruled by **Memory**.

O my daughter, come let us set our wounds on fire
in the mineral springs of miserable mothers.
Who said that death decays a human being?
Your grandmother has become a star in death's night.
                    —*SANIYA SALIH*
                    Syrian poetess

"I, Qamar Yaziji, offer you myself in marriage in accordance with
the instructions of the Holy Quran and the Holy Prophet, peace and
blessing be upon him. I pledge, in honesty and with sincerity, to be
for you an obedient and faithful wife."

They had met on the 6th of January 2014, in a Syrian refugee camp in Gaziantep, Turkey. She had arrived there with her
parents, Qadar and Fouad, fleeing the war in Aleppo. Qamar
would never forget that date. It was her seventeenth birthday,
the most depressing and the most memorable birthday she'd
ever had.

The first thing she noticed about the Turkish social
worker, when he was helping their group get installed, was
his hands and his voice. Two tired yet powerful hands, hands
that seemed to have suffered intensely, but that were still
capable of moving mountains, she felt; and a deep dominant
voice, which left her feeling helpless.

She couldn't but obsess over those hands and that voice—

and the man that came with them. She decided that she had to talk to him. She had to shake one of those hands, let her thirsty palm touch that exhausted skin, a skin so drenched with stories to tell. She had to feel that voice wrap her in its potent texture and blazing tones, like wings of flesh and blood that would fly her anywhere. Absolutely anywhere.

Today, only four months and three days later, they were getting married. Those hands and that voice are going to be hers, only hers, from now on. The vows have been exchanged, even though they didn't have to be,[48] but he wanted it that way. The contract has been signed; she is formally his wife. His Halal. The officiant was already reciting the Fatiha. *"Bismillāhi r-rahhmāni r-rahīm Al ḥamdu lillāhi rabbi l-'ālamīn Ar rahmāni r-rahīm Māliki yawmi d-dīn...Ameen."*

He was the first man she'd ever fallen in love with, and the first person ever to show her rigorous attention. Rigorous to the point of obsessive. Just like she liked. Just like she needed in order to feel reassured.

Not a single detail of her time or thoughts would go overlooked by him. She was also tremendously attracted to him physically. The only thing she didn't like about his looks was his hair. But that wasn't important. "Nobody's perfect," she told herself.

Before she met him, she thought that she was a 100% lesbian, having been strictly drawn to girls. Girls who all made her suffer and neglected her. "Replicas of my mother," she would describe them. As it turned out, she was bisexual.

....

48 Muslim couples do not generally recite vows but rather listen to the words of the imam who speaks about the significance of the commitment of the marriage, and the couple's responsibilities toward each other and Allah. The bride and groom are asked three times if they accept each other in marriage according to the terms of their traditional marriage contract, or Nikah. Then they sign and the marriage is sealed. However, some Muslim brides and grooms do choose to also exchange vows.

◇ ♡ ♤ ♣

"But I prefer the word pansexual," she told her friend Moodi one day. She had watched a YouTube video on her cell phone that morning and heard a pop star define herself that way in an interview. For someone who criticized twenty-first century civilization as much as she did, Qamar was strangely hooked on twenty-first century tech tools. Also, like many Arabs from her generation, she drew most of her cultural notions and references from the "Evil West." An organic product of Satellite TV. She was, in that sense, a civilian representation of the inconsistencies that the infamous *Da'esh* (ISIL or ISIS) manifested: Archaic views and methods disseminated with ultra-modern communication platforms. ISIL displayed a performative contradiction: Their statements refuted the conditions that were allowing them to be stated and spread.

Moodi was a young Syrian from Al-Raqqah, a city on the northeast bank of the Euphrates River, whom Qamar had met during her first week at the camp. He was gay, definitely 100%, and had opted to alter his real name, Mohammad, which didn't go well, in his opinion, with his sexual orientation. The first time he was sucking a man's dick, and the man started moaning: "Oh, Mohammad! Yes, Mohammad! Go on, Mohammad!" he immediately felt the urgency to become Moodi.

"I thought he was going to shout *Allahu Akbar* when he came in my mouth! It was such an erection killer!" he confessed to Qamar. Moodi was funny and kind-hearted.

He was jubilant when she told him she was having a thing for the camp's coordinator. "You beat me to him, you mischievous Eve! And you dare to accuse us of taking all the good ones! Just kidding, *ya albeh*![49] Good for you, sister! You will soon discover the awesomeness of being fucked by a

....

49   Literally "my heart" in Arabic, one of the ways to address someone you love.

179

man. I bet that after that, you will make a U-turn and become completely straight!"

"Maybe I'm just a gay man trapped in a lesbian woman's body," she'd joke with him.

Moodi was the only one she had told about the wedding, once the date had been set. He said he wanted to be her bridesmaid. "There are no bridesmaids in Muslim marriages, you silly! You mean witness."

Soon afterward, he was found dead near the camp's gate. Completely naked. His throat was slashed and his genitals were heavily mutilated. The words "*Louti Hakeer*," dirty fag, were written in dark red on his forehead. With his own blood. The blood had dried and formed a crust. Qamar ran to her fiancé in tears. "They are saying that an ISIL member hidden here has murdered him!"

"There are no ISIL members in the camp, *sevgilim*.[50] Relax. Most probably it was a jealous lover who wanted to push suspicions away from him. That is how the majority of those people die."

Qamar didn't like the sound of "those people," but she said nothing.

"Besides, now that you are about to become a Muslim, you should stop sympathizing with such an abnormality. May Allah help them heal." He said "*shouzouz*," the word that had made her cry herself to sleep so many times back in Aleppo. But she loved him. "Nobody's perfect." The tremendous emotional security she felt with him was way stronger than anything else. She never confessed to him that she had been with women. That she, too, was "abnormal."

Tomorrow, they were going to Istanbul. "It is my mother's birthplace. You will love the city. You remind me so much

....

50   Turkish for "my beloved."

of it. You both have the same kind of wild beauty." They will do so many things together, and travel to so many places. After his work in Istanbul is done, he will issue her a Turkish passport and they will join her family in the US, where they could live for a while. Then he would like to come back to Turkey and start his own NGO. He loves helping people in need. That's what he said, and a voice like his could never tell a lie. He was so passionate that she sometimes felt he would be willing to die for a cause he believes in. "Such a noble soul." They will have kids—at least four—and she will devote all of her time and energy to raising and taking care of them. Then, maybe once they've all grown up and gone to school, she could start fulfilling her own life's passion in her spare time.

It was neither fashion, like her mother had wished, nor dentistry, like her father had wanted. Qamar's dream was to fly planes. Actually, her original dream had always been to become an astronaut, ever since she had watched an interview with the first and only Syrian spaceman, Muhammad Faris, on Syrian TV many years ago. He was from Aleppo, too, and he went into space in 1987. She knew it was a far-fetched dream. But if he did it, she could do it, too.

But that was before the war. Before Gaziantep. And most importantly, before him and this. Now, she has downsized her ambition to flying planes.

"Our children have to grow up here, not in America," he told her repeatedly. She liked that he was a traditional man. Traditional *and* religious. Well, sometimes too traditional and too religious. But that's O.K. "Nobody's perfect," right? She'll sand his edges over time. Besides, she's never been a practicing Christian, to her father's desolation, so she might as well become a good Muslim. One has to please at least one version of God somehow. "Just in case."

"Will you wear the *Hijab* for me?" he asked her right before the ceremony.

"I would do anything for you, my love," she said, while adjusting the veil on her long black hair.

"Absolutely ANYTHING."

⌐

Gaziantep—Friday, May 9, 2014

I won't tell her about the marriage. Nor about Istanbul. She's already gone hysterical when I gave her the news of the engagement last month. She doesn't deserve to know anything about me anyway. She never loved me. She would go to Beirut and leave us for weeks. And she has cheated on my father. Not once. Not twice. Repeatedly. He told us, and she never denied it. Besides, whenever she was in Aleppo, she'd spend the entire time working. Her and her sacrosanct boutique. "It's essential for you to have a career ya binti!"

"No, Mother. Not if I have to neglect my kids because of it. Not if I have to leave them wondering why they were unworthy of my attention. Not if it would make me unable, or unwilling, to cook them one single meal. Not if I have to leave them with a nanny who attached more importance to the latest Kathem al-Saher[51] song than to them. A nanny they would once catch their father shagging in the kitchen at night, when their mother was on one of her precious business/pleasure trips.

"What kind of a mother is that, Mother dear? Didn't anyone tell you that pricy gifts and electronic gadgets don't make up for abandonment? That two weeks of a fancy vacation per year cannot replace a whole life? Screw progress and equality and the West and the twentieth-century woman that you're so proud to be. The progressive twentieth-century Arab woman has been lucky. She's

....

51   Famous contemporary Iraqi singer.

had an old-fashioned mother. One that bathed her and fed her and taught her how to tie her shoelaces. One that stayed up and watched over her when she got sick. It is that woman's twenty-first–century offspring who got botched, because they had a selfish bitch for a mother. Or is it you who overdid it in the bitchiness domain?"

So many times I wanted to shout at her: "I know what you've done back in 2004!" But I never did. Instead, I chose "Bekrahik, I hate you!" minus the explanations. I felt it would make her suffer way more.

I had recently turned seven and Miss Hadia was our second grade English teacher. My first crush, she was, even before I understood what a crush meant. I used to write her silly poems, which I never showed her. I became first in English only to please her. She had been raised in the UK, by a British mother and a Syrian father, and had come back to Aleppo at the age of twenty-seven to study Arabic. She sustained herself by teaching English at our school. She was blonde. Blonde like a hesitant love declaration.

It was a Thursday. Thursday, the 22nd of January. I remember it well because we were off from school and I had seen a show that morning on the Discovery Channel about the history of planes. It was then that I discovered some of those who were going to become my heroes: Charles Lindbergh, Antoine de Saint-Exupery, and of course, the great Amelia Earhart. The show was broadcasted right after a documentary about the Chinese New Year, which was celebrated on that day. Father and Mother allowed Boulos and me only two hours of TV daily, but the nanny would let us watch it as much as we wanted in their absence, to keep us out of her way. We were among the first homes in Aleppo to install a satellite dish.

It was early evening. Mother had just returned from work, and she was in the shower. I happened to be in her room. I was trying some of her high heeled shoes on. She had so many. Her phone was just lying there. It beeped, so I looked. There was a new message icon—the closed envelope—on the screen. I checked the name of the sender. It was just a mysterious H.

Something was urging me to open the phone. It was a Nokia, just like my friend Titi's, the one she had gotten for her eleventh birthday. She had taught me how to unlock it and play Snake on it.

So I did. The message was in English.

"I miss you. I miss our short getaway in Beirut. When will I see you again? Please reply. Your silence is mortifying. Love, always."

I didn't understand all the words, but I knew what "love" was. I registered the number showing under the message on a piece of paper, deleted the SMS, then put the phone back right where it was, on the bedside table. My heart was beating so fast I thought it was going to explode.

"Can I go to Titi's?"

Titi—Tania—was four years older than me. She lived next door, and I used to spend a lot of time at her house. Her parents were very rich and they showered her with all sorts of toys. She had the largest collections of Barbies I had ever seen. And she'd let me play with them.

Mother shouted back from the shower, "Fine! Just make sure you close the door behind you."

She never suspected anything, that day nor afterward.

"Titi, can I use your mobile for a quick second?"

"Of course!"

I dialed the number.

"Hello...? Hello, who is this?"

It was a familiar woman's voice and accent.

Hers.

[5]

QADAR, AGAIN

"Have you gone mad?"

Qadar couldn't believe her ears. Her daughter's irresponsibility was reaching new heights. Ever since they had finally escaped the siege in Aleppo last January and made it safely to the refugee camp in Gaziantep, her foolishness had become insufferable. But this was way beyond foolish.

Where was Fouad, now that she needed him? As soon as they settled in the camp, he had to leave again. First to Aleppo to sell their house—the only asset he had left that wasn't completely damaged by the shelling—then to Beirut to try and get them visas to the US. He took his wife and his daughter's passports with him. It made Qadar feel very nervous, to be without a passport; sort of trapped. But there was no other way.

He had decided they would go to Durham, North Carolina, where Boulos lived. Their son had finished his undergrad and was now a first-year student at the Duke University School of Law. Just like he wanted. Two of his role models were Duke alumni: the journalist Charlie Rose and *Sophie's Choice* writer William Styron. Boulos even got a full scholarship, which was timely, since Fouad's financial situation had gone downhill after the start of the civil war in Syria. He had invested all of his money in real estate, and the properties he had purchased over the years, as well as his clinic, have been destroyed during the multiple bombings of Aleppo.

"Only a few weeks in Gaziantep, then we will head to Durham," Fouad promised. They would enter the US with visitor visas and start the immigration process from there: that was the plan. The Obama administration had recently promised to take in more Syrian refugees, and Boulos had read in the papers that World Relief Durham was being very efficient in refugees' integration. "I've been promised a job for you at a dental clinic owned by a Lebanese American in a nearby city called Hickory. It's a beautiful small town with a pleasant climate just two hours away by car from Duke. The WRF will surely help you get settled there. And Qamar could do a biology major at Lenoir-Rhyne University in Hickory if she's planning to go to dental school later."

It won't be easy to obtain a US B2 visitor's visa, obviously. However, an influential Lebanese politician, one of Fouad's father longstanding *Za'im* friends, had promised to help him. But he's been gone for three months—"The person you are calling is currently not available."

He's never been available anyway, Qadar would shrug every time she'd try to reach him on his cell phone and get the voice message. Could something have happened to him? She couldn't deal with such a prospect right now.

How did we end up here? she kept asking herself since day one. It mortified her that, upon their arrival in the city, they couldn't even afford to rent a miserable room. Rents in Gaziantep had become expensive due to the flow of refugees, and Fouad had almost no cash left. Neither did she. They had to go back to the town's outskirts and stay in one of the camps guarded by the Turkish military.

If one looks at a Syrian refugee camp from above, they discover a sea of white tents exuding optimism and safety. Everything seems organized and neat. A haven where people flock to be saved, to be provided for and taken care of. Not exactly a dreamland, but close enough in such difficult circumstances. One must assess a given context relatively: Gaziantep versus Aleppo, not Gaziantep versus Stockholm…

But turn those white tents inside out like pockets, shake them, and the blackness will fall out. You see the mud in the trails and in the arteries. The threads where people's exhausted laundry hangs like life residues. The tear stains on the used pillows. The improvised schools where a one-eyed orphan is supposed to learn how to count to ten. The timeworn cooktops where women take turns brewing something they need to believe tastes like coffee, or hope. The cold. The unbearable cold in winter. And then the heat. The intolerable summer heat.

Turn the refugees' faces inside out, too. Those faces, especially. You see the shame, the desperation. The disgust. You can't possibly miss the "I wish I had died instead" or "I wish I'd never been born at all" expressions. A forsaken limbo where the only tool of survival is in thinking, "It could have been much worse," comparing their situation to that of those who've been less fortunate. Luckily, in a refugee camp, one always manages to find the less fortunate. Even if you've lost two kids and an arm, there will be someone around who's lost all of their family and both legs. You just need to look close enough, to be a good disaster hunter. For the tragedy of others is your sole consolation.

Two dirty mattresses, a couple of rough wool covers, and a few plastic cups to get drinking water from the dispensers scattered outside: that is all that Qadar and her daughter had now. And it was amidst that desolation that the stubborn and belligerent seventeen-year-old announced to her mother that she was engaged.

"Engaged?! Is this some kind of an April Fool's prank? How and when did this happen?"

"It's none of your business!"

"Your father is going to have a heart attack!"

"No he won't. He'll understand."

"Understand what? That his daughter, who's still a minor, has decided to get engaged in a glum refugee camp?"

"So what? It's not like we will live in this place forever."

"Right. We won't! We are going to the US, remember? What will you do then? Stay here with him?"

"Of course not. We will get married, and he'll come along. We've already figured out everything."

Qadar was distraught. Could her daughter be any more gullible? She was thinking and acting like a spoiled little girl who imagines that as long as she wants something, it can and will happen.

"Who is this man? How did you meet him? What's his name?"

"Again, none of your business!"

"I can't even know your fiancé's name?"

"Why would you want to know? So you could steal him away, too?"

Steal what? Whom? How? Qadar was feeling completely disoriented. Lately she had been seeing her daughter in the company of a social worker, and she did not like it. First, because he was Turkish. Secondly, he looked distinctly older. In his thirties, if not more. Could he be the mysterious fiancé? He must be. It surely can't be the only other guy she hung out with, her noticeably gay friend Moodi. Too noticeably.

"Tell him to watch out, he could get hurt. There are lots of cavemen here," she kept warning her.

Please no! Anyone but a Turkish guy! Qadar thought. She was in fact willing to die in Aleppo rather than come to Turkey, if it weren't for Boulos' supplications and Fouad's assurances that they would soon leave for the States. Fouad never agreed to go to Lebanon, and she had to capitulate. Her daughter already knew how much she reviled this country and its people. "Maybe that is exactly why she might have gotten engaged to someone from here."

"So you could steal him away too?" she'd said. What's with the "too"? What did she mean by that?

"What are you talking about? What's this nonsense, Qamar?"

She had yielded long ago to her daughter's rejection of the name Qayah. Qadar only called her that in her own head.

"I hate you!"

Qamar threw the usual grenade and stormed out of the tent, leaving all the questions behind, unanswered like a sterile mother's prayers.

Qadar couldn't help but cry. She has been crying a lot lately. It was already a very emotional experience for her to be in Gaziantep—"Aintab" as they used to call it during the Ottoman period. This is where her beloved grandmother was born. This is where Qayah had lost her family, her child-hood, her dreams, her ability to smile. In another scenario, this could have been Qadar's homeland, but now she's had to enter it like a beggar. She had to flee death the other way around. From Aleppo to Aintab. A perfect circle of fire, with a circumference of one hundred years.

Qadar kissed the steel locket that hung around her neck. "Help me, *Tatiky*." Neither Boulos nor Qamar inherited hers and her grandmother's red hair. She wiped her tears and went out of the tent to try and find her daughter. She had to talk to her. To try and make her realize what a big mistake this was. "Don't get back at me by getting back at yourself." She also wanted to give her the locket as a token of truce.

Even though Qamar never cared about her mother's side of the family and its history, she couldn't be cold-hearted to the point of not appreciating such a precious and meaningful offering. She knew how much Qadar treasured the locket. She never removed it, not even when she took her kids swimming at the Ras al-Bassit beach, back when they were little and she could still take them places. Ras Al-Bassit was one of the most picturesque spots on the Mediterranean: a wide bay with clean water and clean sand, surrounded by mountains and green hills. She would spend two weeks every summer with her children in a private chalet there, to make up for her frequent absences during the rest of the year.

Qadar was feeling weak, and her knees were quivering. She remembered she hadn't eaten anything since the day before. A few steps ahead, she bumped into him. The potential Turkish boyfriend. He had a stack of food vouchers in his left hand. He immediately placed his right hand on his chest:

"*Assalamu Alaykum*! How are you, Mrs. Yaziji? I'm the camp's chief coordinator. Please let me know if there's anything I can do to help you be more comfortable."

He spoke a fairly decent Arabic, with a hardly noticeable accent. The classical Arabic though, not the Syrian or Lebanese dialects. He sounded nice, but something in his eyes bothered Qadar. They looked cold to her. Cold and empty. She remembered her Aunt Najat's eyes. The eyes of a zombie. And he didn't shake women's hands, which was also quite alarming. A possible indication of Islamic radicalism.

"That's kind of you."

"My duty, Mrs. Yaziji."

◇ ♥ ♤ ♧

"Qadar. Just Qadar."

She couldn't stand being called Mrs. Yaziji. It represented everything she was not.

He smiled. "My duty, Qadar."

"What about you?"

"What about me?"

He flinched for a second. Then he understood what she meant.

"Oh! Forgive me! Beshir. My name is Beshir…"

Another bad omen, she thought. *All Beshirs are criminals.*

"…Beshir Kizlar, at your service."

Lightning. Goosebumps. Nausea. *Please let it be a coincidence.* She has been imploring a lot lately. She didn't know whom, but still, she implored.

"Thank you."

A dry, barely audible thank you.

He was already starting to turn and walk away, having felt the shift in her vibes. Qadar gathered all the courage she had in her. *Not so soon, Beshir* Efendi.[52]

"Kizlar, you said? I read something once about a certain Beshir Kizlar Agha. But I can't remember what or where… in a history book maybe?"

"Oh, you must mean my great-great-grandfather!"

It was not a coincidence, alas. Can fate be any more sneering? Qadar could almost hear it disdainfully laughing at her, "You miserable puppet!"

"He was a war hero in the Ottoman Empire. I've been named after my grandfather who was in turn named after him."

Qadar turned livid. She couldn't help but hit back.

"War hero?! From what I recall reading, he was more of an assassin. I am of Armenian descent, you know!"

....

52   Turkish for "sir."

191

He flinched again. As if he was hesitating between being offended or regretful. Showing anger or empathy. He chose apologies. But Qadar felt it was more out of calculation rather than remorse.

"I am so sorry. You are right. There are always two sides to every story."

"Aren't you from Adana?"

"Yes. That's where I grew up. But my father moved to Adiyaman, in the southeast, eleven years ago because of work, and we never left."

"And what does your father do in life? Is he also a war hero?"

She was clearly being sarcastic, but it didn't seem to provoke him. He grinned. Out of goodness or shrewdness? *Am I being a paranoid*? she wondered.

"Both of us work for Borusan Oto. It's part of my mother's family business. My father was the manager of their Adana-Mersin facility. They sent him to Adiyaman in 2003 to establish their BMW dealership for Southeastern Turkey. I was a fresh business graduate at the time, so I got involved in the process as well. But I took 2014 off to do humanitarian work and to practice my newly learned Arabic. Borusan is one of the few companies in Turkey to have a sabbatical policy for their employees of more than ten years…"

Another grin from the Efendi.

"I don't want to be in the car business forever, anyway. I'd like to follow my own calling one day."

He was giving her more details than what she had asked for. Why? Was it because he had nothing to hide, or the opposite? Liars tend to blabber, too. Qadar's thoughts raced in her head. *His family has money, so I must be wrong about him being an extremist…But then again, Osama Bin Laden was filthy rich, and look at what he did…*She forced herself to stop analyzing. *O.K., enough with the foreplay. The bull's horns. Let's get this over with.*

"So, you are friends with my daughter, I hear?"

Again, he didn't seem perturbed at all. As if he was ready for the bullfight.

"Actually I wanted to talk to you about this. I've been meaning to come visit you properly, but Qamar wouldn't let me. She asked me to wait until Mr. Yaziji came back from Aleppo."

"Talk to me about what?"

Her attitude had become clearly aggressive. No need for the politeness game anymore. She had to push him away from her daughter, and fast. She had so many reasons to do it. But Beshir wasn't intimidated by her increasing hostility.

"I am in love with your daughter and I want to marry her."

His tone was respectful, but also firm. The tone of someone who's telling another: "This is how it is and you have no other choice." Qadar, however, had too strong a character to submit to any underlying menace.

"Marry her?" she lashed at him. "Surely you must realize that she is too young to get married. Not to mention that you are also too old for her."

"Love has no perfect timing, Qadar."

Lightning and goosebumps again. Why did he have to say *that*?

That's when Beshir realized he still had his wool cap on. In his courteous tone, accentuated by the classical Arabic he was speaking, he apologized.

"It is so cold that I keep forgetting about it! Please excuse my rudeness."

He quickly took it off. The last thing that Qadar saw before losing consciousness was his hair.

A pure, deep, flaming red hair, just like hers.

Aintab—Tuesday, April 1, 2014

"Truth is stranger than fiction." So true, Mr. Twain.

I tried to talk some sense into Qamar tonight, but she threatened to kill herself if I stood in their way. And now I am left with the hardest question of all: My grandmother or my daughter? Which one of the two Qayahs do I owe more? Retribution or absolution? Which of the two closures is closer to justice?

Neither.

Hate extinguishing itself in revenge is cowardice. And hate turning the other cheek is self-deceit.

What would you have done, Tatiky? Does his family deserve a hundred years' pardon? If I were to plant my teeth in his neck right now, would I taste your mother's blood in his veins, or her oppressor's?

I am related to this man...I am related to this man.

I need to keep saying it in order to believe it. Sometimes I feel that our hearts and minds misunderstand each other on purpose, conspiring against our well-being. An old prostitute once told me, "One should always follow instinct. Neither sentiment nor reason. Both lead to doom."

Don't feel. Don't think. Just dance with what you do not know. What we do not know is our only real ally. Our lifeline.

 REUTERS

Istanbul female suicide bomber identified

JANUARY 8, 2015 / 6:28 PM

ISTANBUL - The female suicide bomber who has blown herself up in the Turkish city of Istanbul on January 6, killing one police officer and injuring another, has been identified, officials say.

Qamar Qaya Yazigi, as the refugees' records have shown, was a Syrian citizen from Aleppo. She has targeted a police station in the tourist hub of Sultanahmet, near the Blue Mosque and Hagia Sophia museum. Dressed in a niqab, she has entered the police station and told officers she had lost her wallet before detonating the bomb. She was five months' pregnant, the forensic pathologist declared. Turkish Prime Minister Ahmet Davutoglu had told reporters that the bomber was carrying two other devices, which were safely defused by officers on the scene.

Yaziji, 18, a Greek Orthodox Christian converted to Islam, had married Turkish citizen Beshir Kizlar, nicknamed Abu Sayyaf El Adanawi, in May 2014. Kizlar was an undercover member of the Dokumacılar terrorist group linked to ISIL. He had briefly worked as a coordinator in one of Gaziantep's refugee camps, which is where the couple had met, Istanbul governor Vasip Sahin told Reuters. They first spent three months in Istanbul, from May to July 2014, before entering Syria. In Syria, Abu Sayyaf El Adanawi fought for ISIL and was killed in Kobani last November, at the age of 32. Yaziji, who was pregnant at the time, was sold as a sex slave shortly after his death, before escaping and irregularly reentering Turkey.

The Dokumacılar are allegedly formed by around 60 or 70 Turkish citizens from the Adıyaman Province, situated north of Gaziantep, who crossed the Turkish-Syrian border to join ISIL and receive training in ISIL camps.

The woman bomber's mother has been located and notified. She flew in from Beirut this afternoon and identified her daughter's shredded remains, mainly from an old steel locket she had around her neck. The mother has made no statement to this date.

Epilogue

My grandmother survived the Armenian Genocide.

Well, almost.

She was born in Aintab (also known as Antep or Gaziantep, situated in southeastern Turkey) to an Armenian father, Nazar, and an Armenian mother, Marine. The Markarians were one of many families forming the city's large Armenian community back then.

One ominous day of April 1915, when she was merely three years old, the Ottoman soldiers forced her parents and hundreds of thousands of Armenians to abandon their homes. They marched through the Syrian desert, without food or water, and many were harassed, tortured, raped and massacred. More than a million people died. She was one of the survivors.

"Survivor" is a big word. My grandmother committed suicide in Beirut in 1978. She was sixty-six, I was seven. She ingested rat poison. I saw her lying on the kitchen floor, white foam coming out of her mouth. Every time I think about her, that is how I see her: Not holding me in her arms; not telling me a story; not stroking my hair or giving me a thousand kisses, the way a grandparent should be remembered. No, I just see her lying on the ground, lifeless, and screaming all her unsaid, painful words in my head. So, you see, she did not really survive the Armenian Genocide. Like many other victims, she was killed, only with a bit of delay: A time bomb was planted in her heart and soul on that sinister day. Tick. Tick. Tick. It exploded decades afterwards.

The wars' undead are either living cadavers, or deferred casualties.

⤙

My grandmother was born in 1912, my mother in 1946, I in 1970, and my eldest child in 1992. I am half Lebanese, a quarter Armenian, and a quarter Circassian, but I also have Syrian and Palestinian roots. When I discovered all the diverse bloods running in my veins, I finally understood why I've always been at war with myself, *within* myself. Is it a coincidence that the forefathers of the man I love are Turkish from Adana, where the massacres had begun? I hope it is, almost as fervently as I'd like to think it is not.

I sometimes picture all of us together, people with different ages and ethnicities, worshipping different gods, speaking distinct accents and languages, trapped in a long, interminable tunnel of successive conflicts. A doomed melting pot called the Middle East, which has witnessed and is still witnessing more struggles, adversities and hatred than could ever be told, from Armenia to Lebanon, from Palestine to Syria, not to mention Iraq, Kuwait, Egypt, Yemen, Turkey… The list goes on.

Often have I wondered, growing up experiencing and seeing so much violence and sorrow around me, if this hopeless region was forever predestined to be a land of hurt. Between the ISIS mercenaries slashing throats today and the Ottoman soldiers spreading horror a century ago, what has changed, really?

I was raised in one of Beirut's Armenian ghettos. My grand-mother's house was nearby, and I used to visit her almost every afternoon with my mom. She was always sad, even when she was smiling; especially *when* she was smiling. As if she felt she wasn't entitled to joy. She never spoke to any of us about what she had gone through during the Genocide. I can understand why. I still find it extremely hard to talk about most of what I have experienced during the Lebanese Civil War, a war that ruined my childhood and adolescence (and countless others'), and which aftershocks are still ravaging both my homeland and my soul. I've never told my kids about the horror on the streets, the terror in the shelters, the slain youth, the constant state of anxiety, the open wounds that are buried in me like land mines.

After my grandmother committed suicide, I asked my mother to teach me Armenian. I wanted to learn her language. Until this very day, every time I speak Armenian, I feel her heart beating in my chest.

I've dreamed about writing this novel as a tribute to her ever since I can remember, but for a long time, I've lacked the courage to do so. It seemed like a leap in an active volcano, one that I wasn't prepared, or maybe willing, to take. Why now? Because for some mysterious reason, I felt the urgency one usually feels right before it is about to become too late.

And so, I leapt.

I've often found History—as a study of the past—to have shortcomings despite my appreciation for it. In History's dry language, victims become statistics, predators become conquerors, profiteers become winners, homes become blocks of concrete, birthplaces become pieces of land forfeited or seized, and distress becomes a conquest or a defeat. Neglected are the orphans, the bereaved, the widowed, the raped, the beaten, the abused, the homeless, the displaced, the shot, the slaughtered, the injured, the dead. Neglected are the innocent sufferers from all sides, those who had no say in the calamities they endured. "Collateral damage," they are called, and History's ("His Story"?) wide angle camera moves on. But those, in my criteria, are the real war heroes; those we can only see with the heart's microscope; those whom we find, most often than not, told in "Her Story."

My admiration for combatants, some of the alleged supermen of Mankind, was stillborn anyway. I was barely six years old when I first saw one "in action." He was tying our neighbor, a kindhearted Muslim man called Hussein, to the rear shield of his BMW with a rope. The man was still alive, screaming and twisting, when the car started running down our street. Down then up. Up then down again. At one point Hussein fell silent and his corpse became a dead weight dragged by the car. Many of our quartier's residents were standing on the balconies of their apartments watching, as if torture was an entertaining, innocuous family TV show. I felt nausea. I felt shame. I felt outrage even without understanding, then, the why of it all. Later in life I understood, and the feelings of nausea, shame and outrage became even more justified, added to a sense of responsibility. These became the fuel of my lifelong struggle against all forms of injustice and prejudice. Hussein's only crime was to have been a Muslim in a suburb of Beirut where Muslims were seen as the enemy. I am sure that in a parallel dimension, a Muslim girl has witnessed the same atrocity being done to a man whose only crime was to have been a Christian in Beirut's Muslim suburb.

By which standards did violence come to be considered a form of heroism? Beyond the philosophical notion suggesting that Man is inherently evil, it would be hard not to link this praise of violence, at least partially, to the reality that so many of this Earth's gods are power obsessed, revengeful and blood-thirsty, and even worse, glorified for being so. Evidently, I am not saying it is the gods' fault: We cannot blame the creature for how the creator has designed it. Those gods are but a re-flection of what is worst in our species: Instead of overcoming fear we opted to idolize it. Instead of transcending the vicious part of our nature we decided to justify it with divine models. One glaring example of that is how, in the Middle East's dominant religious mythology (i.e. in the three monotheistic religions), the human race has witnessed a fratricide ever since its firstborn generation.

The sons of Cain and Abel will keep on slaughtering each other until we acknowledge a different genesis for ourselves, and reimagine more humane gods.

Or no gods at all.

—

This book has been a challenging exercise in "predicting yes-terday." However, it made me realize how imagination can sometimes be a more loyal biographer than memory. Because, at least to me, human experiences and feelings are and will al-ways be more significant than the events that triggered them. The scars outweigh, and outlive, the knives. The narrative is loosely based on my own family's history and geography, but most of the life events, key dates and details belong to fiction.

What's fiction anyway but a pending reality?

I have enough intellectual integrity to not pretend that my outlook on the conflicts narrated in this work is an objective one. I do not believe in human objectivity anyway; nor do I have a great deal of respect for the notion of neutrality. I have written this novel with my own flesh and blood, I have dug into the past and present with my own anxious nails, and I am too directly involved in all four wars and their damaging consequences, to be anywhere near having a "neutral" position. While I know that a so-called fact is, most often than not, one side's fact, and while I am well aware of the controversy, debates and different—often contradictory—viewpoints related to the Armenian question, the Palestinian cause, the Lebanese and the Syrian wars, I have consciously taken a stand from each and every one of them. Simply because this stand is the story of my life. The gray areas of history, the assertions and denials, the opposing versions of the opposing parties, were not my concern at all while writing. Only the human and personal dimensions were. While the general political opinions might differ, the individual suffering remains the same, whoever the culprit in each conflict was, and whatever its motivation or course have been. The victims are all alike. They are never victorious, even when they belong to the triumphant side. They see the eyes of the opponents' victims in their own mirrors. They hear their cries and know that the tears are bursting out of the same abyss. They are expected to bear the losses and stay silent, holding their pain inside; a pain that eats them bit by bit, like a cancerous tumor or a demonic possession. In these pages, I wanted them to unleash their words like a raging storm and achieve a double exorcism: for me through their stories, and for them through mine.

I am no idealist. I know that wars can sometimes be necessary, or inevitable, or useful even. But they can never be just. There can't be a "war on terror," because war *is* also terror.

And a war can never be really won. Not as long as one innocent life is lost because of it. Period.

I never found out the real reason why my grandmother had an Arabic name. Her Lebanese identity card—a document I hold on to like a treasure—states that she was called Jamileh (meaning beautiful in Arabic). Both her parents were Armenian, so it would have made more sense for her to be called Siranush or Siran or Sirun (Armenian versions of Jamileh) or any other Armenian name. Over years of asking around, I've had different, sometimes confusing answers from family members. One told me that it was not unusual for Armenians in Turkey to give their children Arabic or Turkish names. Another one asserted that her name had been changed in Aleppo where she and those who survived from her family had fled after the start of the genocide. A third one claimed that it actually happened in Beirut, where she and my grandfather had come to live many years into their marriage. Finally, I reconciled with the enigma. There were so many unknown, missing pieces in Jamileh's life puzzle anyway. So many "lost years." What I cannot know, I shall reinvent.

But then again, can I really take credit for "inventing?" Hardly. My entourage is packed with women who fought wars and women who endured them with stoical courage. Women who lost love and women who lost family. Women who have been forced to choose between two punishments; two darknesses, each bleaker than the other. The Christian immediate cousin whose name should never be mentioned because she ran off with a Syrian Muslim. The Palestinian distant cousin who committed the crime of marrying an Israeli Druze. The Armenian friend who got ostracized because she dared to fall for a Turkish man...

We're all Blood Queens. There is a bit of Qayah or Qana or Qadar or Qamar in all of us. In me too. In me especially.

This made-up family memoir is an homage to them and to all those who paid, are paying, or will pay the price of being born into lands, religions and ethnicities they did not choose. For we shall keep on paying up until the day when the future would have reimbursed all its debts to the past, in this big-bet Poker Game called Life.

—*Joumana Haddad*
Beirut, summer of 2017

Characters

♦

Qayah Sarrafian: April 11, 1912, Aintab – April 11, 1978, Beirut
Aslan: Qayah's half-brother from Beshir Kizlar Agha, 1916, Adana
    – unknown
Avi: Qayah's love, 1911, Jerusalem – 1948, Ramat Rachel kibbutz
Bassem Barakat: Qayah's husband, 1894, Jerusalem – 1982, Beirut
Fadwa: Qayah's mother-in-law, 1872, Jerusalem – 1947, Jerusalem
Fatima: Qayah's second daughter, 1948, Marwahin – 1954, Marwahin
Grigor: Qayah's adoptive father, 1862, Moussa Dagh – 1924, Jerusalem
Hosanna: Qayah's favorite sister, 1900, Aintab – 1915, the Syrian
    Desert
Marine: Qayah's mother, 1883, Diyar Bakir – 1916, Adana
Najat: Qayah's third daughter, 1954, Beirut – 2007, Beirut
Nazar: Qayah's father, 1873, Aintab – 1915, Aintab
Negan: Qayah's best friend, 1912, Jerusalem – 1948, Jerusalem
Shafik: Negan's father, 1890, Jerusalem – unknown
Vartouhi: Qayah's adoptive mother, 1870, Moussa Dagh – 1929,
    Jerusalem

♠

Qana: Qayah's eldest daughter, March 2, 1946, Deir Yassin
Khaldoun: Qana's love, 1936, Beirut – 1983, Beirut
Luqa Barsom: Qana's husband, 1943, Beirut

Qadar: Qana's daughter, September 24, 1970, Beirut
Fouad Yaziji: Qadar's husband, 1965, Latakia – unknown
Boulos: Qadar's son, 1992, Aleppo
Omar: Qadar's love, 1960, Beirut
Nina: Qadar's best friend, 1970, Beirut – 2012, Beirut

♣

Qamar: Qadar's daughter, January 6, 1997, Aleppo – January 6, 2015, Istanbul
Beshir Kizlar: Qamar's love, 1982, Adiyaman – 2014, Kobani